STORIES INSPIRED BY

SIOUXSIE

GREGORY PATRICK

No part of this work may be used without the written
consent of the author.

ISBN: 978-0-6151-6508-0

Published by Orotund Multimedia Publishing
copyright 2007 Gregory Patrick
gregorypatrick.blogspot.com

FIRST EDITION 2007
All text and graphics by Gregory Patrick
Cover Design: Orotund Multimedia Publishing

For my niece, 'Misha Folaji.
May she always be inspired by strong
women.

INTRODUCTION: DEAREST SIOUXSIE

Dearest Siouxsie;

There are many of us who consider you the ultimate queen of influence. You moved yourself onto the music scene when women were deemed unsuitable for political endorsement, when women were excluded from the front lines of musical putty. While other girls spun their hair up in teased honeycombs, you shredded yours to highlight the kabuki style face make-up that made your stage shows so enticing, but even more so, you proved that art was dismissive, and when urged, submissive to your power.

I recall seeing you perform live for the first time at the Tempodrom in Berlin in 1988 (or was it '89?) while promoting *Peepshow*. You approached the stage bare armed in a top hat, slinky black dress that shied just slightly from miniskirt, and long satin, black gloves. I stood directly before you in the front row throughout the show and remember distinctly your involvement, not with the band, not with the audience, but with the over machismoed security guards before you as you slapped their heads, butchered them with some chosen lyrics, and ultimately rested a leg atop a monitor revealing something beneath your dress only they could admire. Your brilliance was delicious....and throughout the episode you told the audience while applauding to "Hush!" Your empowerment was provoking and inspiring. That evening I smoked a cigarette for the first time. I catalogued you often, and found myself deeply moved to your music from that moment forth.

As much as I am fan of the SOUND of Siouxsie and the Banshees (and The Creatures) your exemplary lyrics are what have held me even until now; the slightly twisted, poetically bent prose you wrap your vocals around. For years I found myself absorbed in the more cinematic soundscapes of some of your music, often finding myself closing my eyes and seeing a visionary completeness to your words. Ultimately, I found myself scribbling these visions into print, then retracing your music again, scribbling more and composing stories.

I am fully aware that some of your work has been influenced by literature and, therefore, this work of mine seems a redundant full circle landing nowhere near where your tracks were influenced. But, that's to be rightly so.

Should not the mark of an artist be their ability to take a thought, a moment of eureka and make it distinctly their own? All praises indeed to the gentleman whose book prompted you to score *Red Over White* but, indeed those lyrics, that sound, the overall mood and consequence it may have on the listener lay squarely on you.

Over the course of the last ten years, I came across track after track that compelled me to write and a number of short stories emerged. Songs like *Rawhead and Bloodybones, Nightshift, Voodoo Dolly, Tenants, The Last Beat of My Heart, Skin, The Sweetest Chill, This Unrest* and *Are You Still Dying Darling?* are just a fraction of some the songs that pressed me into scribbling. I had never quite fully realized the exact moment, nor the exact method in which to publish these stories until I saw a calendar and realized that your birthday was approaching, a milestone. But, then again, to someone who is timeless, what is a milestone?

Although I hope that this work will be read by many and those that read it find a new interest in your work and in mine, I consider this volume distinctly for you, a gift on your 50th birthday. May this book be a representation of the influence your name, your music, your style, and your distinctness has had in not only sound, but fashion, visual art, and animal rights.

To this chanteuse I offer the gift of how she has inspired.

Happy Birthday,
Gregory Patrick

27 May 2007

Webs to Weave Yourself Around

About Siouxsie Sioux:

thecreatures.com
thebansheesandothercreatures.co.uk
(the absolute best resource for info on Siouxsie)
untiedundone.com
myspace.com/siouxsie

CONTENTS

ICON

GREGORY PATRICK

I was a legend.

For many years I had made my name synonymous with deceitful horror and bitter madness. I had scripted story upon successful story acquiring not only accolades, but a small fortune and fame worthy of any popular musician. I had managed to swell the imagination of my readers with gruesome, albeit fictitious tales of the most perverse sort. These tales, born in the darkest of hours, complete with alcoholic induction and self deprivation, made my name famous, made my image a recognizable, iconic profile to be respected. With a sly smile, well beyond intoxicated, I would conjure from within my own dereliction scenes of betrayal, murder, and viciousness. In the process my fans became as addicted to my pen as I had become to the bottle. My fans desired more and more ink-filled pages of hell's best description. In-between publishing my audience grew more anxious, as I grew more and more restless with the madness I had helped to perpetuate.

I had lost the need and the desire to bring blackness into the world, had lost all need to fill this life with the most unholy of ramblings and set out to acquire and capture a new audience of intellects and thinkers who would challenge my brave political thinking, or who would spend countless hours in debate. From mine own hands I required writings that would stand along the lines of the most notable intelligentsia, writings that would dispel all the previous poisons I had murdered bookstores with.

My publisher scoffed at my intentions and insisted that I continue on my successful path as a demonic warlord, as a wordsmith of grotesque perversity.

"This isn't about art and intellect," he prophetically told me, "this is about money. This is a business. There is no place for art in business."

With my urging, and my threat to find a publisher elsewhere who could capitalize on my name, I convinced my publisher that the pitter-patter of my heart needed to do something real with the talents that God had laid upon me. I was able to convince this industry man, whom my own fortune had helped to create, that I needed to be set free.

And as he suspected and forewarned, my endeavor was a critical disaster. My fans fled in droves from my new work, and more agitated than ever, moved so far from me and my once infamous name that my publisher insisted immediately that I return to my previous style or face financial ruin. I found no fondness in this decision, but the ego's need to return to the paramount of my own game was the deciding forces that lured me back into the world

STORIES INSPIRED BY SIQUXSIE

of gritty, hellish prose.

I set out immediately. My next work of fiction was a forceful rebirth back into the genre that I had helped to create, reinventing the standard of which I had tried to escape. In my own consciousness this was nothing more than fodder for pivotal dollars.

The tremble of my words echoed forth across my old readers as they quickly returned to the bright red font my name had once claimed. Gone forever more and never to return was my need to reach the intelligentsia. I was now back in the arms of the common man's horrifying psyche, as he paid me well for my ability to bring him to his wide-eyed, smiling madness on a daily basis.

What I find in hindsight and what is so regrettable about this situation is that when I learned my new work made it to the bestseller lists I did not rejoice. I was thankful for the money, yet imprisoned was I, in a style of writing that kept me closely locked around a bottle of whiskey and kept my spirit in deep despair.

Can you understand reader, what it must be like to spend every waking moment of the day, hands dripping with the crimes of criminals? The heart pushed away constantly all feelings of love and desire, and the ego in almost cartoon fashion sought a daily myriad of punishments for which to inflict upon itself. And why? For the sake of money! For the green's sake, I spent my greatest moments of life under a cloud of ever increasing darkness, spent my days under the spell of my own ability to fictitiously put on the page the

21

description of beheadings, slashed throats, and self induced abortions.

And all of that was about to change....I was about to be set free.

One evening, sitting before my typewriter, and with whiskey bottle held tight in clenched white knuckles, I scripted a most desolate tale of a one room school house set to flame, torched and burned to the ground by the teacher of the institution herself....after having locked all of the children inside. With a need to describe the red hot timbers gone embers just *exactly*, I would reach again and again for the bottle of whiskey at my side, would pace into the center of the room on occasion with lit cigarette. And once the tale was finished I moved to the couch in my parlor to relax, to do nothing but witness the birth again of money-made madness.

I sat there in my parlor, sat there with bottle in one hand, cigarette in the other, slouched and slumped between the envelopes of the sofa cushions, eyes growing weary, any faint smile finally subsiding....and I content that fame and money were to be handed to me for my lowliest of endeavors.

Then a strange and sudden, although dull sound was heard to my left. It was a tunneled sound, the muted echo of a noise similar to shredding metal that slowly morphed into a near and recognizable screeching. It was then I turned to see with eyes bleeding, and broken teeth screaming for help, the sight of a small child surrounded by flames. With horror I watched this young thing, only 5 or so, pulling at her own burning hair as it singed quickly between her tiny palms, watched as her lips bubbled and melted, distorting her shriek into a dull drone.

She shook her head violently, the fire tearing away her flesh and baking her exposed bone as she clung to the wall now nearly a small skeletal mess as the muscles and tendons in her short frame melted to the floor in small piles of fire, reaching for me, crying for me, calling my name and begging for help.

I let forth from my belly an unknown sound, not quite scream, not quite horrified denial, dropping my bottle of whiskey and racing for the bathroom, grabbing a towel, wetting it quickly, then racing it back to toss upon the already burned alive little girl.

However, the room was now dark again, as it should have been, all hint of fire gone....no residue of burn, no torched carpet....no little girl. I held the wet towel in my hand, water dripping from my elbow to the floor, frightened only by my mind's quick inability to ration between real and dementia.

I walked slowly to where the girl had been, where I had watched her burn alive before me, her screams echoed only in my head.....as though nothing had happened at all. I could only make the strange attempt at a nervous laugh, pick up my spilled bottle of whiskey and sit again on the sofa.

For some moments I sat thinking only of what may have

caused such a vision, from what in my own fanciful thoughts would have brought about such an apparition? The answer was obvious, for this little girl set afire before me was nothing more than a clear and concise detailed description of what I had cleverly typed out on my machine earlier. And just to prove it to myself, I stepped into my writing room to see it boldly on page three. There, resting, and waiting to be engulfed by eager readers was the description of the little girl, just as I had seen it moments before. But, from what within had caused the thing to be seen so well by my eyes? Why had she appeared so wickedly real before me?

Back to the sofa I went, the soft cushions of the sofa again surrounding me, the gulps of whiskey now sloppy, and I alone in a darkened room nearly crying. I sat the bottle down beside me and rested my head in my hands, covering my eyes and suppressing the sanctity of tears.

As thoughts of imprisonment and depression swarmed through me, I caught a glow through my fingers; a warm, orange glow that grew steadily brighter. There, in that quiet and dark domain did the great light of fire once more begin to show itself, the roar of the inferno increasing, getting louder. My eyes widened, my fingers separating to reveal what vision my mind now tricked me with: my silhouette cast against the wall, surrounded by the flickering hues of red and yellow, of a fire behind me where I was forced to quickly turn.

This time it was a young boy. With one glance that became a stare I knew I was familiar with him, for I had given him his death on page four. Yet, instead of his demise on the page I was forced to witness it in my parlor, running back and forth before me, pulling at his own jaw, slapping his own body with panic as the fire ate him quickly. Now his face, his young face dripped and slid slowly from his skull as he screamed for his mother, as I let loose tears upon tears and screams of my own. Here his skull fell into his quick step, his teeth dropping with flame from this toddler's wrecked cackle, he dropping to his knees, falling faceless first into the carpet, the fire caking every cell in his body into a morbid pile of twisted, burned bone.

I could take no more of this, would accept no more of this and raced for my front door to find the handle suddenly ignite like a lit match before me. It was then I heard the door to my writing room shut swiftly, and the sound of the latch being locked. The sound of the boy's crying had gone, but still there was the burning remains of his corpse, the sound of that fire catching onto the carpet, the draperies, sending me quickly into insanity.

But, what was this in my writing room? What now did my mind have in store for me? Who was this there? Slowly, I stepped toward that room, hearing something faint moving inside, hearing a rustle, a movement, a thing in there, a someone making a racket. My mind ignored, my heart disputed that my living room was now on fire.

I stopped outside the door of my writing room to hear louder than the crackle of the burning fire the sound of someone typing. Alas, there were no pauses, no solid sounds of someone making a conscious attempt at words....but a mad rambling of the keys quickly merging into one another.

I grabbed the handle, knowing full well that it was locked as the typing stopped briefly. I wanted out of this, wanted my madness to cease, wanted to set an end to this evening quickly. I pushed against the door, and again the rapid fire of the typewriter keys with machine gun brutality began again. I pushed again, and again, and again, slamming by body forcefully into the door until finally it gave way.

The sweat from my own panic and fear had not even time to hit the floor before turning into vaporous steam when revealed to me was a woman at the typewriter who said to herself whilst wildly typing, "At once there was one, then two, and now the number increasing to five, now six....and when he looks back again, the number of burning ones in his parlor had amounted to twenty, perhaps even twenty-one."

I heard a roar behind me, the fire growing instantly greater, and turning round to look into my already burning parlor was perhaps twenty, or as she had mentioned, twenty-one small children crawling, burning, reaching for safety and screaming at me for help.

Back to the woman went my eyes and with my heart falling into tragic rapidity. I knew who she was, had conceived of her myself, had penned her hair in a bun, had penned her dulled floral print dress, her smokey, charred laughing roar that ignited its own fire in my belly. This was the teacher from my precious tale, the woman who had set the blaze that had killed every child in that locked one room school house.

I screamed, "STOP IT! STOP IT!" Yet, I was not speaking to her, but to my mind, insisting that if I closed my eyes the visions plaguing me this wretched eve would be done for. But, this would not be. For she was still there, the children were still there, dying now so close to me that I could feel their burning, could see the pile atop one another as they came close and died, and another climbing on top of the dead one to get to me, and he or she, too, succumbing to the flames.

The teacher, however, did not look at me as I screamed for the consolation of Christ, as I begged for the mercy of the devil's dancing about my limited existence, my soul clinging between sanity and profanity. This mad woman kept right on typing in a crazed manner, never once looking at me, never once removing her eyes from the pages after pages she ripped from the machine with haste, only to begin a new one.

Running to her and picking up the pages as they fell to the floor, I could she she was penning my every action, my every subtle gesture, my emotions, my speed, my sweat, my reactions to the children, my own self doubt about my sanity.

I could take no more of this, and if to be burned alive was what my art had required from me for betraying it, then so be it. I had had enough and was done for in mine own eyes, cared no more for survival, and fell to the floor at the teacher's feet crying, sobbing, eyes peering to heaven, admitting my demise, ready to be consumed by my own fire.

To my right I spied the pile of burning children, when one was burned alive, another would take its place in repetitious rebirth of vision. I crawled to them, my sobbing a sad thing, my hands reaching for them, my body getting hotter.....I grabbed them, held them, my skin being set aflame, my tears evaporating as quickly as they shed. I held the little girls and boys, hugging onto them, clinging to them and begging for forgiveness, I falling completely to the floor as they climbed onto of me, screaming and crying out for help, the pain of the fire reaching my mouth and lips and eyes was no consolation at all for the pain I had introduced into the world.

And that was the last I remember before waking again. My hugging those children as they died, my crying as I clutched them tightly to my chest.....

I am now a nearly unrecognizable mess. My skin was so badly damaged by the fire that now, even months later, the pain has not gone and a constant ooze of bleeding still surfaces over my entirety. I have one eye for which to see, and even then, it is nearly melted shut. My lips were burned away by the fire leaving my mouth continually open and dry...my tongue, freshly healed by the blaze by this point, is only half its original size and in order to speak, I must do slowly and with such a pace to make the words understandable.

I no longer write anything, for my hands were burned together into clumps of skin that are unable to be removed from my own chest. My audience is gone, of course, and on occasion, I hear on the news programs the tragedy that befell me. As they turn my tale into one of severe doom and of an icon's misfortune I try not to allow tears to spill from my one eye, for the salt in the tears causes my face to burn with pain.

They report that I had let a cigarette unattended and passed out whilst the fire engulfed the extent of me and my home, nearly killing me in the process. They use official papers and documents made by fire marshals and experts in this field, and there has never been any cause to doubt it.

Alas, I know that's not true. I know what happened to me was real...for it is to the teacher I dictate this, and she who types it out for you to read.

GREGORY PATRICK

a LETTER TO MONICE

GREGORY PATRICK

My Dearest Monice,

In the blackest hour of the night, the moonbeams reflected a paleness onto the graveyard's pebble stones that crunched beneath my feet. It is only by this fraction of light that I was able to guide myself. My hand held tight about the shovel whilst the wind smothered me coldly, yet, I persisted past the tombs and charnel markings, breathing hard and slightly grunting as some wounded animal. Though my course through the cemetery was to be secretive and silent, the steps I made broke through this nocturne's disturbing quiet and I was forced to walk upon the graves, walking where the wind lingers and where the remains of diseased men lay sleeping eternally beneath the soil.

The grave I sought was of no ordinary man, but a vile and scorning creature who acted in the most wretched forms of discipline, whose thoughts of pleasure came from the sight of your pain and whose only need was to watch the tears willfully spill from your blood strained eyes.

He had stood approximately four feet tall in his living days and had some eyes that I can only describe as popped; large and wildly wide. Yet, here is where the horrors of this man's affliction begins to question fact. Horns, they had said, and even some sort of protrusion of hair on the backside that gave the insulting illusion of a bushy tail. There were said to have been five teeth in his head, three above and two below, aiding to certain areas of his story that tell of him gnawing the arms and legs of his victims to a bloody stump. This dead man that I sought, whom I had begun to think grotesquely fabled, was said to have had the most atrocious hands: long fingers with claw-like nail endings that grappled men and women with the tight grip of an arachnid.

His deformity had been by birth, but before his death, supposed death that is, he had acquired some disease whose medical name escapes me. It was a dreary unease that caused his skin to grow thin, so thin that you could watch the blood of this creature, the veins (both blues and reds) wrapping about his odd body and twisting through his brittle bones. You could even see the brain, they claimed, plotting monstrous things beneath the skull. The transparency of the cerebral membrane was apparently so vivid that the gray matter of his mind called to you with devious intent.

I was anxious to find his corpse, anxious to rip apart the earth, for the sight of his rotting bones would provide astounding conclusion at long last, finality to my own trepidation, and would determine the security of my future. The sight of his decaying remains would solidify whether I might live or die.

In order for me to correctly convey to you the terror behind this tragedy, I must confess to you that I was a rotten child. I was always involved in the worst kinds of pranks and would throw wild fits of rage when denied whatever I wanted. This was much to bear on my father. With such a devotion to his career and with no wife to help raise me, for my mother died giving birth to me, I was left throughout the first half of my life unpunished for my bad words and bad deeds.

Now, when I was twelve years old my father was reported missing. The investigations ran for some many months until at long last his body was found at the bottom of a wishing well. He had been strangled with a rope. No suspect nor murderer was ever charged and the haunting thought of no one to blame sent me reeling towards an eternal mistrust of man.

I was sent to live in an orphanage run by some Benedictine nuns until my eighteenth year. It is here in this cold and drafty place that I learned of the acts of punishment. My sly ways were quickly corrected by the backsides of hands, or the broken ends of sticks. But, by the time I left the orphanage I was a proper young man who did no malicious thing, nor spoke unjustly of another. I met your mother when I was twenty years old and soon we married. You were born two years later and we named you after my mother: Monice.

Here is where the strange slants in my story begin to unfold.

On the day that you were born one of the nuns from the orphanage came to pay your mother and I her respects. But from her lips came the most unsuitable advice. She said that when you should behave badly your mother and I should punish you roughly, so roughly that you should wish death on us. Hardly the things to say on such a day of living praise. The nun continued to warn us, saying that neglect of your punishment would do nothing but invite grief, that we would cut our own throats if we did not strike at you for the mildest of misbehaviors. I did not remember her name, but remembered well her stings and lashes when I misbehaved as a child. And these things I wished never to bear upon another, let alone my only child, my only holy one.

Two years after that visit you behaved just as I had, Monice. As I, Monice, you were just as rotten a child, forever unscolded for your behavior. And I? I never found it within me to harm you, to punish you rather, for your ill manners. Even though you did behave so wildly, and even more so at the age of three!

At this point the nun returned yet again with the same odd request.

"I'm nearly at the point of begging you to be firm with your daughter..."

I would not have invited her in had she not brought to mention my father's death and the man who was responsible for its doing.

Having halted her promptly at the door, a twisted grin fell upon her holy chin and she said, "I remember you being a lad, being torn by your father's death. Let me help you put an end to that madness, dear. Let me tell you what happened to your father. Did you know that he was at our orphanage, too?

"Some years back, well before you were born, when your father came to stay with us, we gave our basement to a man named John Michael who performed for us in a most unusual manner. He was our," she peered skyward, whispered a quick prayer through tight teeth, "our punisher, you might say, who disciplined the children for us."

For the next three hours I listened with so biting an intrigue at what had happened within the walls of that orphanage, and was even further transfixed when later my father's name came into play.

A deformed character answering to the name of John Michael, after having been ridiculed and taunted for his deformity, sought refuge from this world in certain wishing wells in our town. One spring one of the nuns from the orphanage sat at the edge of one of these wells wishing for happiness in the world. While tossing the penny into the blackness she stumbled upon eyes. She called to them and asked them if they were hurt, but the eyes replied, "No, I am only hiding. I too, wish for this happiness, but will wait here in my abyss until this happiness has been achieved."

"But, don't you understand," insisted the nun, "that you

37

must strive with your ways to make this world a better place? You must take action instead of solitude. I will help you out of this well, dear brother!"

The nun gathered her sisters and when they pulled John Michael from the murky bottom of those depths they immediately understood his reason for being so wary of man. He was horrid to look at; the most perverse of any malignancy they had ever witnessed. His eyes were too large for the head that they nearly fell out of the skull, and the hair on his bottom, so thick and course and long, and his teeth so few in the head, so wretchedly brown they appeared as those of a demonic rabbit. And the fingers, poor man! So long and so boney that they were not at all pleasant to view, as though tentacles with claws, and the skin, gray and thin exposing his intestines, his mind, his heart!

But, in their beauty and charm the nuns could see no deformity and offered him their basement in the orphanage for which he could apply his hiding from vindictive eyes.

At this time in the orphanage there was a debate swinging and growing bitter daily. Half of the nuns were against the striking of a child, and the other half thought it was the best possible way to change his disrespectful days. Then one of the nuns started plotting processes in the mind that can indeed lead to penalty...

On a Sunday in winter one of the boys was behaving badly and the nun watching over him had grown quite impatient with his sour display.

"If you don't stop this madness right now and behave yourself, I'll...I'll...."

Here came the test. *Try it now!*

"I'll take you down to the basement!"

"Fine! Take me to the basement! It's too cold out here!"

The child laughed in the playground twist, the snow falling onto his even colder smile.

"Ahh, but, do you know what is down in the basement? Obviously not! There is a monster down there with the taste for living flesh, who is always begging me to bring him a nasty little boy for supper!"

The child then began to claim that the nun would surely go to hell for such lies. Then the nun, in such a wonderful display of aggression, picked up the child and began carting him off the playground, his little feet dragging in the snow as he fought and clambered so.

Within seconds, nearly strangling the boy as she struggled with him, the nun pulled the boy into the orphanage, down the long corridor at the farthest end of the building, and down the steps that led to the basement. The child did nothing but fight and shout how he did not believe in monsters.

But there, just before the cellar door though, did he begin to wonder, for at his height he could peek through the keyhole and there staring at him was a huge, blue eye. And on the other side of the door he could hear the heavy thud of improper breathing; wrangled breath that it caused the imagination to go wild in the tot's little mind. The breathing sounded as though there was something stuck in the monster's throat. *A bone perhaps? A small piece of a boy who also had misbehaved?* Coughing and muttering were beginning to sound from the other side of the basement door. *Hunger! The taste of a boy who had been naughty, something like a craving! An addiction!*

"Sister," asked John Michael through the most grotesque tongue of raspy, heavy sputter, "have you brought me a friend to play with?"

The child began to cry and plead for forgiveness, but the nun still felt that the boy had not quite yet learned his lesson.

"Don't struggle like that!" She shouted to the boy, "He will only want you more!"

And with that she threw open the door and there stood John Michael in all his deformed glory. The child, his heart nearly ceasing, screamed a shriek unlike any noise ever known to have penetrated the ear of man, ran up the staircase to his bedroom and crawled beneath his bed where he stayed for a fortnight.

And the child was a perfect angel henceforth.

Success, thought the nuns! They would never have to strike at a child again! When one grew in need of a lashing, they would threaten him with the hungry "monster" in the basement.

This successful system of punishment worked for sometime...until John Michael took to abducting the little boys by night. Oh, yes, if they had been bad they would be taken down to view the sight of the John Micheal's monstrosity, but later that night, John Michael would creep up the staircase, return to that same little boy and would carry him down to his lair...and there he would perform unspeakable things. Their miseries screamed unimaginable things...and these vile things are far to wretched for me to discuss, much less pen for my daughter.

The nuns finally caught John Michael in his trickery, alas, only after two years of this mad practice had been made upon the babes, only after two years of the most grueling sadistic torture had been performed on the little boys in the middle of the night. Their young minds had been damaged for good. Their eyes no longer shined, the smiles no longer the promise of childhood.

The nuns, terrified at what they had provoked, beat and whipped the disfigured man in a rage of guilt and shame. His skin was too thin to withhold the lashing, though, and he fell to the floor dead.

The sun was coming, people were mingling on the abbey grounds, and the children were beginning to wake. Later that night, they would remove his remains in a hard cardboard box, they agreed. And sure enough, some moments after midnight, John Michael was laid to rest at the dirtiest edge of the cemetery with nothing more than two twigs fashioned into a cross to claim as his grave.

Here is where my father, your grandfather, Monice, enters the situation. My father had been one of those boys at the orphanage and many years later, after I had been born, he began to complain of this stalking and perpetual watching. He returned to the nuns now a grown man with the beginnings of his own family, complaining to them that he felt John Michael was still alive and out to get him.

Paranoia, insisted the nuns, and nothing more. They had rid themselves of John Michael with their own hands years before, had chored through the process of burial themselves. They knew beyond any shadow of doubt that the creature was dead.

Then why did he have this feeling of threat? There was someone in his room when he slept, he could feel it. And there in the corner at any moment was the disturbing shade just slightly bolder than black of a four foot fellow. Petrified, he would shiver without wink until morning.

Not long after my father was reported missing and was soon found dead in the well. It is not at all chilling to report that it was the very same wishing well where John Michael had first been found.

One by one the boys returned to the orphanage pleading for assistance, claiming they saw him still, not directly, but the

42

flickering image of his remains when they should turn a corner, the hair on the backside as some trail for their eyes to frighten upon. And when sleeping, yes, they knew he was in the room. They could hear that heavy, thud walking beneath the bed or even worse, they could see the reflection of moonlike tombs upon those huge, blue eyes in the darkness.

One by one they experienced a stalking, went to the nuns for assistance, received no help whatsoever, and died horrid deaths not long after.

But, only some of them returned, the nun told me, not all. Only those with undisciplined, unpunished children returned with pleas for help, while those with perfect little angels for boys and girls were left unbothered and untouched.

This lead to the conclusion by all that John Michael was finally out to snag the parents of those children who had not been disciplined; John Michael was still the punisher in his own mind, keeping the boys, now grown men, in perfect check. He was finally correcting in his own twisted way this unhappy humanity that had led him astray.

The nun finished her story, begging once more for my own safety that I punish you severely, for no reason at all, but this very instant to go forth from my parlor, find you, and beat you to the point of death.

The nun left my home when she finished her story. And I

did not believe.

Then soon came my own trepidation. I, too, began to feel that ever present presence of something odd in the corner. And when turning to peek would see only the rough remains of something darting off quickly. When sleeping I heard the breathing, suggested to my wife we were in danger, and she, too, convinced of fable did not believe. Within days I could no longer sleep, could no longer think, for there was the constant shadow over me of some impending doom of which I knew was forever in the room about to strike at me. It became unbearable. Intolerable. Still, I made no effort to punish you... and the stalking I had been told of by the nun did nothing but increase to a degree that hinted at impending death.

I went to the graveyard of the diseased tonight, though. With shovel in hand I set out to prove to myself that John Michael had been a fable.... and that I was in no danger of threat.

I found the little edge of the cemetery with the frail code of sticks and began to dig for hours and hours. Through that time I saw only the clever shadow of that wretched man over there in the corner, here beneath an old oak tree, or there at the cemetery gates where the smell of the grave lingers slightly longer. And when I came to the cardboard box, I opened it to find not a corpse, no, not at all, but something even more terrifying. A box of books.

I knew him to be real now. I knew him to be so deceiving. When the nuns took out to the cemetery that box, they took out not him, but the weight of binding, papers, and words.

I ran home as quickly as I could, though I knew it was too late to prevent any harm to myself, much less save your mother.

I found you in the middle of our brightly lit parlor, your eyes clenched closed, your screams dissolving my blood to nothingness...and there in the corner I saw what would sooner or later be true: your mother dead, held lolling, head rolling to the side, and mouth and eyes wide with final fear as some discarded doll or hideous plaything.

The police have come and gone and no promise has been made to me of a suspect. Like so many years before, when my father died, the mistrust of man has begun to swell again.

It is now two hours since my return from the cemetery, and there in bed you now sleep whilst I write out this letter in haste, applying the instructions that it should be given to the nuns, to be given to you upon the birth of your own child. I beg of you, Monice, to do what is asked and told of you, and when your child is born, my darling dearest, love him or her, but more so, do not neglect your child, but punish them if need be. I cannot ask forgiveness from you for what I am about now to send you to: a continuing snare of entrapments that will forever rotate in a deadly cycle if you do not take this warning.

I love you dearly, so dearly, words will never ever fully penetrate the emotion onto the page. Know that I will forever love you. Forgive me, I can say nothing more for I can hear John Michael approaching....

With the utmost in regret, I pray this night may save your soul one day.

Your father.

THE dOLLY

GREGORY PATRICK

After having learned of the horrors inflicted on my two good friends, I am no longer able to trust that foul creature called "woman." Dripping with such damned deception, this tale will rise slightly short as to why I hate the female kind. Some of them are heartless, and yet, some of them behave so helpless. But, whichever sort of that slender species you prefer, I assure you she causes my stomach to twist and turn with the churning of burn.

Now, if I may proceed to the incident that caused this terrible unrest.

My good friend, Steven, was waiting in the belly of a certain grand old home in Savannah, waiting for an eager lady he had been enraptured with, waiting with growl in his breath as he muttered to himself, "Will she be here like she promised she would be?"

Hovering before him was a staircase that rises high, branching into the two separate heavens of the house. He stared at both wings descending with a piercing curiosity and an adoring perplexity as though she might at any moment saunter down coyly, for never had a woman's footsteps so intrigued him....for they were sly, silent footsteps so very much the rhythm of his heartbeat.

49

Alas, it was the portrait of Miss Elizabeth, the damsel in question, that caught his attention out of the corner of his view and he turned with mesmerizing pull to see her caught on canvas. Elizabeth pleases, surely, and the painting only appeases a sudden rush of her gush, not nearly as fatal as feeling her flesh. With a longing commencing in the groin and colliding with the heart Steven was overcome with a need to touch the unbelievably life-like oil portrait. He raised his palm in jest and commenced to feel the painted flesh with caress.

"Have you lost your mind, Steven? Or are you really that hungry for me?"

Startled by the rolling of her voice (a rolling I have only known tigresses to make), Steven turned with embarrassment to find Elizabeth at the top of the farthest staircase, one hand supported at the hip, the other hand playfully sporting a very long cigarette. Divinely the eddies succumbed to her, wrapping about her and presenting her as some sinful gift.

Now, it must be said that a dashing man of Steven's kind could have had any woman about his arm. But, this woman had an awesome quality about her that some had thought shameful. And it must also be confessed, that although Elizabeth was an extremely beautiful woman, it was this shameful quality combined with a clever controlling of the tongue that made her irresistible to men. Steven smiled, went to her, planting his lips firmly at her neck's nape.

"You're early," she said.

"I wanted to get here before the storm hits. Is my brother here yet?" The question came through kisses and pecks placed delicately about her long neck.

"No, not yet. But I assume that he will be." She giggled. "Tonight's the night! Shortly, he will walk through that door, run into my arms, lick my poisoned lips, and fall dead at my feet. And then this house will be yours and mine. I've read the will, refused to sign a prenuptial. It's done, darling. God, what work I had to go through to make sure he would do it! Sleeping with him! He may be your brother, but that man is a BORE in bed. Oh, and laughing at his stupid jokes. Keep going, darling, don't stop!" And Steven bit heavier into her neck. "I had to pet him, you know! PET HIM! Your brother prefers to be petted in bed, like some ghastly child! Oh, but I don't care anymore! It's all going to be mine! More, Steven, more!"

But, he did not continue, and instead pulled away softly and simply said, "Ours."

"I beg your pardon?"

"You said it would all be yours. It's to be ours."

Startled, as if caught with a lie she struggled with the simple word, "Y-y-yes! YES! Of course! HA HA! OURS!"

It was all so very true, all this confessed. None of them held simple pennies to their names, but all the riches and all the fortunes that their eyes beheld of late belonged to Steven's brother, Justin, whom as you may have now summed was about to marry the sly Miss Elizabeth.

This spider bitch had set her spot and had commenced weaving her silver plan.

Steven pulled Elizabeth into the living room and poured them both drinks. Giving the fine crystal glass to her he said, "Shame to have to kill him, though. He's not been the best brother, but the only one I've had."

"Darling," she went to his side with the slight makings of a pout, "you know how everyone dislikes poverty. Especially me. You're poor, my love! And so close to having it all! You're so good looking," caressing his face, "and so solidly built," grabbing now his biceps beneath his crumpled coat, "and so very....ha....well rounded in bed. But, this poverty thing of yours cannot be overlooked! Now, I know what life has been like for you being in his shadow and all. I have done what I can to skim money from him and give it to you. But, I expect strong and noble men like you, darling, to be desperate to make a change." Now she turned stern on him. "I expect the man I am with to be good looking, built, good in bed, and *wealthy*....Do I make myself clear? I expect you to carry out this plan you contrived."

"But, this was your idea, for my benefit."

She put the drink down and sat on his lap, "For OUR benefit." The woman again giggled with an evil tone.

Then he asked her, "Are we greedy?" His hand moving along her thigh....

"Yes!"

"Are we evil?" The hand now making its way beneath the hem of her skirt.....

"Yes!"

"Are we sinful people not worthy of heaven and its angels?" The hand, dear God, the woman did roar once his hand finally arrived at her prize.

"YES!!!!!"

A sudden jangle of keys was then heard and the two of them quickly fell wide eyed with haste.

"STEVEN! QUICK! Into the closet! Don't make a sound! This is it!"

"I'm putting the poison into the wine! DO NOT DRINK THE WINE! Do you understand? DON'T DRINK IT!"

Steven reached into his pocket and pulled out a smile vile of white, shiny, reflective powders. After pouring the deadly additive into the drink, Steven then crept into the closet close by, leaving a small crack so he could witness his own brother's demise. Only seconds later did Justin appear in the living room.

Miss Elizabeth then went about her performance. "Why,

Justin! I thought you'd never get here!"

Justin noticed her dramatic panting, her hand across the cleavage, her heart puttering so wildly that her pulse was visible through her chest.

"What on earth is the matter with you?"

She now noticed her own nervous anxiousness and worked '*demure*' beautifully to its own honor.

"The storm! It had me frightened! Goodness! Such a racket out there! You must never leave a woman alone in a fierce rage of angles such as this!"

Justin ushered a laugh. "It's a simple summer thunderstorm. Nothing to worry about."

"Still!"

"Alright, alright.....It's alright. I'm here now, my love." He grabbed her and pulled her forcefully close.

"You ought to relax, Elizabeth."

She peered up at him with heavy lids.

"Of course, you're right. You're always right about these things. Well, I imagine a glass of wine would settle my nerves. Would you care to join me?"

"More than life itself."

The foreboding should not at all be attributed to me, for I simply recount this tale as it was told to me. Irony, and all.

Justin moved to the wine cart with Elizabeth following, a

STORIES INSPIRED BY SIOUXSIE

girlishly playful attitude of gushy love.

"Speak up, Elizabeth. What did you do with yourself today?"

"Oh, my day can hardly be thought of as interesting by your standards."

"Of course not. I was just trying to make conversation."

She winced, bit her tongue, her name on the home's deed keeping her anger at bay.

"Speak up. What did you do?"

"What is there to do? I made more wedding arrangements.....which, by this point, seems to not even involve even me. There's someone to handle that, you know. Then I tried to run some errands, and yet again, I met a dead end! Your staff is worthy of every penny you pay them. They had done everything. There was nothing more for me to do, lest I decided upon dusting, which, to be perfectly frank, is beneath me. So, with nothing to keep me company my mind just wandered all day."

She paused. Criminals often flaunt their intentions. "I started thinking about your brother."

"What about my brother?"

"Let's be honest, dear. Winter is coming. Jobs are hard to come by, the economy is wrecked. It's likely your brother will end up a statistic."

"Are you kidding me? A statistic? I never thought of you the political sort. What? Were you polled this afternoon by a newspaper?"

Again, a heavy bite down on the lip.

"Face it. Your brother might starve. Your brother could freeze. Your brother could die." Like, I said. Criminals often flaunt their intentions.

"Elizabeth, you're neither a politician nor Florence Nightingale, so what gives?"

"What is that supposed to mean?"

"It's very unlike you to be worried about anything that does not involve yourself, so what gives? Are you sleeping with him?"

Rage boiled within her! How dare he mimic or mock her, or make her good intentions seem less than extraordinary. She only smiled at him, and behind that smile a massive tension of clenched teeth were grinding into each other. This murder, she thought, was warranted! And in the future, from moments like this, she would remind herself, the arrogant ass had it coming. She handed him the poisoned glass of wine.

He lifted it, but paused before sipping to say, "You've never shown yourself to be compassionate, you know. So, I'm interested. Are you sleeping with Steven?"

Oh, what was he saying! Did she even listen? Did she even care? The thought of that poison so close to his lips was all that kept her steady attention.

STORIES INSPIRED BY SIOUXSIE

"Beth," he said.

"MY NAME IS ELIZABETH! I hate it when you call me 'Beth.' It's lazy and lower class."

Again came the pause, the wine glass so close, his lips nearly touching the glass that time. Her eyes went wide!

"You're good at shopping...," oh, making it sound tedious and unimportant, "....at organizing parties," she waited with eager anticipation, "....and at looking good. Which is what you're best at. Really."

"Oh, just DRINK IT ALREADY!"

Justin summoned the glass to his mouth, took an enormous swallow and gulped down every last drop.

She leaned in as Justin's eyes slowly began to twist into a confused manner. Her malevolence was peering through. Justin dropped the glass, with Elizabeth stopping quickly to catch it before it hit the ground. "Don't break the crystal, darling! It belongs to me now."

Justin, as any poisoned victim might, grabbed his throat with long and twisted fingers that had begun to turn blue.

"What have you done to me, you bitch! I can't breathe!"

"Well, shopping and looking pretty aren't the only things I'm good at! That's death, dear! You feel life leaving you???? You feel death coming! That's what that is!"

If only you might have seen this mad woman so full of her

own hysteria! Her eyes, I swear to you, were so vacuous and monstrous. And all the while, she clutched onto that crystal glass she had rescued from breakage so tightly that one might have warned her it was about to crack.

Ah, but that madness of hers, those eyes just mentioned before were crowned by a smile of achievement as Justin hit the floor.

"How could you betray me, Beth!"

"Eeeeeee! Lizzzzzz! Uhhhhhhh! BETHHHHH!"

"How could you betray me! How could you do such a thing to me? Why would you want to kill me? My heart-," oh, the clench at the chest as death loomed in even closer! "-it belonged," now a gasp! Spitting even, "-only to you!!!"

"Oh, God, how dramatic!" She ran to him, crouched down beside him hatefully. "I wanna give it to you straight before you croak, you ass! I did fuck your brother! And he's so much better at it than you! The only thing keeping him from being perfect is this HOUSE! Your MONEY! Your SHIT!"

The helpless man made some unintelligible gurgled noises as he slipped into death's arms.

"You were the affair, Justin! Not him! *You* were the affair. Thank God, it's over!"

Justin reached for Miss Elizabeth one final time, but fell dead before her feet.....just and exactly as she had said he would.

Not more than a moment passed before she screamed, "Steven! Come out, come out! He's dead!"

Steven did appear almost instantly, the door to the closet flying open and he racing to his brother's corpse, prodding the body with his toe. Quickly he lurched away from the carcass and made some nervous fit of laughter. Truth was now sinking in. The reality of his accomplishment weighing tough on his conscience.

"Dead," he said, as if saying it even more so would make it fictitious. "Dead," as he stepped back, quick visions of the two brothers as boys made their way into slicing gesture into the forefront of his view; visions of when they had laughed together, played together, had been so lovable towards one another. Steven's face turned ghastly white. "Dear God, what have I done?"

"Oh, for crying out loud, Steven! Don't you even think about regret now! It's much too late for that!"

"Did we have to kill him? I mean, maybe we could have kidnapped him! Something!"

"Much too late for that, Steven! Come on!"

She rushed to him, doing her best to calm his hysteria. After all, when wealth is involved, a criminal acting alone fear only the law. A criminal acting with an accomplice need fear the accomplice, as well.

"Listen to me, Steven. Look at me! No, no, no, don't look at him! Look at me and listen. We had this planned from the beginning,

59

remember? He was keeping it all for himself. He wouldn't help you with a dime, wouldn't do anything at all to help you! You had no choice! You would have starved! Do you understand that? You were nothing! So much of nothing! Look around, Steven! It belongs to me now!"

"Us."

She rolled her eyes, "YES! US! You and me....."

Now came her sexuality, that shameful quality that you recall that had put her into first place. Her mouth was now at his, her eyes closed, and her voice rushing into a husky whisper.

"You and me, darling. You and me.....with me.....part of me.....We'll celebrate by being one....oh, God....do you feel that? It's me.....wet....wanting you, so happy for you now that you're perfect. I can help you forget tonight.....it will feel *so good*......so good that what we did here will be forgotten by morning."

Steven smiled as any man ought to have. And all focus and attention was on the sly Miss Elizabeth.

He sighed, indulged himself with the life giving air that was a luxury to him now, took a lung full, then let it out. "Break open the champagne," he exclaimed. "That wine is a trifle potent tonight!"

Mercy, this woman's deadly persuasion was so very contagious! Stephan went to the portrait of his beloved and gazed whilst Elizabeth went back to the wine cart.

"So," said he, now that his manhood was at attention. "tell

60

me more about what you want to do this evening. Start at the beginning."

The body was still where they had left it. It could no longer be referred to as 'the brother, the lover, the monster,' for all those things would have signified that he had an influence, that he had a life....No longer true. Those days of suppression and poverty were over.

"Let's begin at the fire place and wait for this storm to pass." Have you ever heard the sound of an orgasm stretched again and again with the crackle of a perfect fire? That was what she eluded Steven to thinking, as she turned to give him a cheerful smile......

However, she also noticed the small vile of poison sitting with ease from the first deadly drink she had made. Her smile of cheer quickened into a smile of opportunity. And why not? With both Steven and Justin gone to the grave she would have the entire fortune to herself. And who on earth would have guessed that this had been her intention from the start. Share??? Share with no one, being a woman had taught her. Find what you can, keep it for yourself! This included not only men, but homes, money, furs, and yes, of course security! Find them and keep them for yourself! And with luscious men coming to court her and dripping her with all sorts of gems and gifts, she would soon be the richest and most coveted woman in Savannah. Not to mention, her reputation as solitary and such without a man would make her respected in the upper classes. Respected, she thought to herself, with a threatening and fearful seam keeping it all so cozily together.

She poured the small amount of poison left into Steven's drink.

"As I said....Let's start in front of the fire. We'll do some writhing, some clawing........some gasping....."

The woman handed the glass to her unsuspecting victim. He took it into his hands slowly, but with a quick gulp, not unlike that of his brother, he drank it all down, hearing her whisper over his shoulder as he did so, "Careful, you're likely to choke."

And choke he did as he fell to his knees. Elizabeth stood above him, so proud of her tricks!

"This drink," she claimed, "is a concoction of my own! A mixed drink! One part champagne, one part poison, and one part SPITE! I call it the Deadly Beth!"

"ELIZABETH!"

"HOW RIGHT YOU ARE, DEAREST!"

"WHY!!?!!"

She sighed as the man grabbed at her gown.

"Steven! Give me some credit, please!" She pulled her gown out of his hands. "Did you think I could let this opportunity just slip by!"

Alas, Stephan had not the time that Justin was afforded to

interrogate the bitch in her hideous tricks, for he slumped quickly into death, falling over the corpse of his brother.

After pausing only slightly to laugh at the ease of her plan, Elizabeth then began to creatively think on how to discard of the bodies.

Pacing over one limp arm of one brother, then the leg of another, she bit at her highly prized manicured nails, battled with herself even, thinking how foolish she was to not have thought the plan through fully. Discarding of the victims would be a chore! Something like work! Something that would require her to do lifting, maybe even digging!

And then it stuck at her so quickly she said it twice to reaffirm its brilliance.

"The basement! I'll bury the hounds in the basement!"

She placed her drink back at the tragic wine cart and went for Steven, who lay over his brother. And as she flumped him over to his side, she rolled her eyes and then questioned her own plan. Would it not have been smarter to have kept this one alive just long enough to help her drag at least one body down into the basement? Lord, this was going to be a bore, dragging each dead man one by one into the the kitchen, down the staircase and into the basement.....Alas, the selfish ego once again raised its bright eyes to fulfill her with some inspiration. Just think, said this inner fiend who had propelled her to do so much killing in one eve, just think what lay ahead if these bodies should be fully disposed of! What riches lay ahead! Fight woman, fight! For all that you require is but some sweat, a rusted shovel, and six feet of digging away. Elizabeth complied with her ego's praise and carried on with the full fervor of erasing the dead men's remains.

For one hour she indulged with the dreaded chore of concealing her sins, leaving the bodies to rot and decompose into dust until all evidence was degraded.

It is a tiring chore indeed to hide one's sin, and her chosen chore was messy. She took a shower to rid herself of the dirt and grime that had licked her white skin. Once finished, she slipped into her nightgown and crawled into bed. Comfort and rest kept her cozy beneath the covers, dreams of forthcoming parties and all that money to be spent her nighttime companion.

However, a scratching on the window pane kept her from turning out the light at just the final minute. She removed the sheets and stepped from the safety of the bed and moved towards the window. Slowly she stalked within this room towards the danger that lurked close by....alas, her eyes spied beyond the window to find not a thing there and assuming it to be the paw of a dog or the branch of an old tree summoned to animation by the storm, she returned with a spinning turn towards the bed.

But an object with such speed came crashing quickly through the window and landed on her with a heavy thud. The glass poked her, the smell of this thing on her back frightened her and the cold wet hand of a man covered her scream. Tossing Elizabeth onto her back the madman peered down at her with hateful eyes seething a vendetta. It was Steven! Just recently buried, returning form his makeshift grave in the basement! It could not be! Could not be at all! The concepts, the possibilities raced through Elizabeth's mind! He had not drunk enough of the champagne to render him dead, only slightly unconscious and ill, or even, that he had died and that the supernatural powers heard in books and passed about in stories were all indeed true! Dead men do seek revenge upon their killers! Dead men do return!

Consumed with muddiness and bitter disgust he pressed firm Elizabeth's cries with his hands. Ah! but this spider bitch was quick and was not so easily defeated as she thrust her knee into Steven's stomach. The dead man spilled onto his side as Elizabeth scrambled out of the bedroom, racing down one set of steps only to be met with the same wet hate of the other brother, Justin! She looked behind to find the other apparition with stare descend the staircase behind her. They moved in synchronic suffering towards the doomed Miss Elizabeth who begged and pleaded with sighs.

One of the specters, closing in on her, as they approached from different sides, cornering her ironically beneath her own oil portrait mumbled the simple, colloquial, half hearted: "....Beth!"

"E E E E E E E E - L I Z Z Z Z Z - U H H H H H - U H -

65

UH....UH......UH! UH! UH!" Her words now became gasps for air as her back went flat and defenseless against the wall, her hands clutching violently at her throat, the demonic eyes of the dead men peering in closer and closer on her. Her hands now went to the pain in her chest as her own eyes went wide, darting with confusion and fear into the gaze of one brother then the other.....then slowly she went blank eyed, stared quietly into another space and time....crumbled to the floor and died. The two grim demons stood above her.

The specter once called Steven spoke to the ghostly once known Justin. "Feel her pulse."

And his hand went under the already blue hued face of Miss Elizabeth to feel at her jugular.

He replied with something of a smile. "Dammit.... She's dead...."

As they sipped wine later that night in front of the fire they spoke loving to one another as brothers would and as these brothers should.

"Steven! That poison! What was that? Powdered sugar??? God, that wine was terrible!"

"Exactly how I knew she had tried to poison me, too. The champagne was horribly sweet!"

"I won't be able to get that taste out of my mouth for weeks!"

"I know what you mean, brother. With wine it must be disgusting!"

"Yeah, it lingers on the pallet. I have to tell you, I didn't think I was gonna be able to handle being buried. I hated that. I didn't expect her to do all that."

"It wasn't so bad! And besides, who buries a body in three feet of soft dirt! The woman was an obvious amateur."

"The first flood and we would have washed up into the living room!"

The laughter spent some time punctuating their bravado.

"Alright. So that's another one dead. What do we tell the police this time?"

They both glared with some reminiscence and some disgust at Miss Elizabeth's portrait.

"The truth."

"How do we prove it? I mean, we've got to come up with something better. This scare tactic keeps killing them!"

"Who the hell has to prove a heart attack! This one was easy."

Stephan reached for her portrait and pulled it off the sturdy nail above the mantle. With but a few steps he laid the portrait of the now deceased Miss Elizabeth with a stack of recently claimed fatalities, also boasting their proud faces in oil canvases, now gathering dust in the closet. The collection of femmes was now seven.

"Hey, Steven, That reminds me. I need to borrow some money."

"Of course. What do you need it for?"

"The artist. He's doing another portrait."

"Oh, do tell."

"Miss Christine. How does that sound?"

"I can see you now screwing with her head. Christy! Or just CHRISSY!!!"

"I already tried it! She hates it! I LOVE IT! Why is it that you think we attract such demonic women?"

"Because the women we attract are bitches."

And with that they laughed lovingly and chatted the remainder of the evening as brothers would.

Now, it should be perfectly clear of my dislike for women, reader. For the devil is real. And the devil is indeed a woman.

FOR ANNE COULTER

The bitch was a thin thing, skin hanging limp from a boney frame that shamed even the most starved of souls. When *she* smiled it was a sure sign *she* was lying, and when *she* wept it was testament to the happiness of seeing living things dying.

And you couldn't escape her. As much as you despised the grotesque woman you couldn't arrive at a fine night on the town without seeing her walk with skeletal gate down the street. God knows, you didn't want to be brushed up against her for fear of being stabbed by one of those boney elbows....or lest be stuck in a conversation with her about the madness of the the soft hearted. No, *she* wasn't the sort to pleasure you with compassion, but rather *she* was the mean queen of a regime who adored watching simple things that belong to simple people being taken from them. If *she* should come to your home and knock on your door you sat still, you breathed barely and hoped her own boredom would keep her moving on. However, if were you unfortunate enough to receive one of her calls in person you winced when you could behind her frail frame. I often times found myself when near her moving closer to the radiators or fireplace to keep warm, for her very presence was cold, darling....Just cold.

I heard an account of paint peeling at the reverb in her shrill when someone asked if *she* would contribute a penny, maybe two, to a common cause to benefit the poor.

"BAH!" shrieked *she* (and to those who knew her it was considered softly), "My money! Are you kidding me???? You want me to part with my MONEY??? What's the sense in capitalism, of working hard if it's to benefit someone other than me? If God wanted them to be wealthy He'd give them money!"

You see, *she* self-conceived herself as a legend, born from frightening half truths that belong only in political spin. *She* renounced reality, who *she* was, where *she* was from (although no one knew who *she* was, nor where *she* was really from) and brought about an elaborate scheme to seduce the very populace *she* wanted to be a piece of. *She* claimed to have been from an alleged "here" and belonged to these alleged "whose" (although those who had been "here" don't recall her once, and those "whose" can't remember having ever met her). This gave us all something to chat quietly about behind her skinny little backside. *She* was a lie, a fraud, and we unanimously laughed over a bottle of wine when dubbing her with the title, "Queen of the Mean Regime, Social Whore at Best."

Her life would have been extremely anecdotal, the kind of sad tale one tells over gout inducing dinners of which the highbrows are accustomed. But, it was her downfall that made her name laughable by all who were repelled by her. It was an episode, supported by me, that would have made any normal human a martyr. It was because it was *she* that made the whole episode cause a grin to anyone who despised her. And to much of our great admiration, even the common man came to spit at her.

Now, I will admit that most of what has been written so far is my own pure opinion of her. One that is biased at best. I shall try to deal with the facts of her dubious piece of humanity from here on out. I won't admit to her by name, you will and HAVE seen. I won't allow her immortality. Not in my pages, not by my hand. *She* will only be referred to as *She*.

Let us proceed.

There was a country home, an old thing that belonged to a friend of mine who had bought the left alone place precisely for his prized foxes. He adored foxes. "Cunning, gorgeous, and smart!" He had bred a number of them, but did so in a manner in which they retained their wildest of qualities. "Free range," I believe he called it. He did not pen them, did not quarter them into living domestic and imperfect lives against their instinct. He instead let them run free, let them be as untamed as any of God's creatures ought to be.

My good friend had said so many pleasant things about the view from the rural home, so many charming moments when the sun waxed and waned, and what the moon did to the leaves of the trees that hugged the home on all sides. "A place where my foxes get to run free." And as we discussed the pleasantries of a simple country life, *SHE* did appear. (AND GOD, if only you could see the manner in which I stamp out the letters on this typewriter when mentioning *SHE*!!!! *S-H-E*-!). My friend and I were at the corner of two streets, neither of which would have readily expected to see *she* there, but there *she* was, and there *she* spoiled everything.

She comes darting up, looking around as that sort do to see who would see *she* being seen with my friend and me.

"I heard a rumor," *she* said to my friend. "You bad man, what have you done?"

"So....so....*good* to see you," said he to *she* with a fake half quarter thing that didn't quite make it to smile. And then, as respectable as my friend is, said in hushed tones to *she*, "What rumor are you referring to?"

"I heard a rumor you were hiding this beautiful man from me! Hi, I'm-" ...*SHE*!

She outstretched her hand to me, behaving as though I were some new thing never seen before by *she*! Had *she* no recollection of two or perhaps three times before where we had met at various parties around town? Well, thought I quickly, of course the Queen of the Mean Regime wouldn't! Not when there are better people at the party to meet than me! At least three times it has been that I was introduced to her at a party, would take that skinny, cold, boney hand to greet her and only be met with, "How do you do! If you will excuse me, there's someone I must talk to!" And *she* would flee! And me? Feeling rudely brushed would concede that *she* was a mockery of the social scene.

But not this time, not here, not now, not on this occasion, not when there was only me, my friend, some common men stepping about...and *she*. And knowing in groups *she* would be well received decided that we three were a better scene than the dreary team of just simple all alone *she*. Skinny *she*.

Now, one would question why I have such a beef with *she* being so skinny. The answer is one that deals primarily with social acceptance, my friend. The woman refuses to eat because *she* thinks it makes her socially acceptable. *She* thinks it makes her finely desired in the right eye sight. So while people in the world have no choice over whether or not they will eat that night, *she* treats food as a bothersome part of daily life. And that's why I make such a stink of it. People die by the same denial *she* affords herself. I hate her for that....that and skinning animals practically alive. But, I'm getting to that.

"Look at my face," *she* says, "I'm stunned that you've been keeping him a secret from me!'"

"How do you do?" Says I, nearly ready to attack *she* for being rude enough to have forgotten me not once, not twice, but on three separate evenings.

"Much better now that I know people like me are on this

street! ha ha! They ought to keep the poor penned in their own neighborhoods where I don't have to be bothered by them."

People like *she*? Are you kidding me? If I were ever to be people like *she* then I would plead of thee to KILL me!

"So, what are we talking about?" *She* muses.

I know the direction of this game, I know how it can be won, I know how it is played best! Make it sweetly known to *she* that we have no intention of revealing a weekend of perhaps four or more of us friends having fun. But, of course, we would let her down gently, explain its a private affair, one that would require an invitation. And as I lean into her, my mouthing beginning to pucker a first and foremost formal word on a decline, my friend, my FRIEND! pounces quickly in with, "We were talking about this weekend."

No, thought I so shocked that he would even mention it! For mentioning it would require a question from her, that's how this game of manners is played, dear friend! You're allowing her to ask about the weekend so that *she* may invite herself! *Don't let her!*

"Oh? What about this weekend? Is there a party somewhere???"

My eyes grew wide, my heart flittering so fast! Alas, not fast enough to again jump in to save us from *she's* being a permanent fixture this weekend.

"Well, yes...sort of." My friend has no idea how this game

is played. We've lost, we're done. "I haven't called it a party, but I imagine it will end up as one. I have a new home, a beautifully cute thing out in the country that I want to Christen this weekend with friends."

"I would LOVE to come!" *She* says....and what more could be said.

I stood there, so stunned I barely moved while *she* giggled and pinched me. And once *she* was done grabbing at me, *she* reached into her purse for a pen and paper exclaiming, "I must have all the details. Go ahead. How do I get there?"

LIE! shouted my mind, *Just...LIE!* We've lost playing this game with her, but it doesn't mean *she* should be rewarded. Give her the wrong address! Give her something! Give her "one right here, and two lefts on this street" sending *she* into a boggy creek that would carry her downstream to her death....

But, no. My friend was dutiful, giving detail after detail on how to send *she* precisely to where we would be this weekend.

And once my friend was finished giving directions to his beautifully cute country home, *she* showed her perfection cleanly through her too white teeth.

She asks, "Will Mrs. Dandry be there?"

"Why, yes! Yes, she will! Why do you ask?"

"Well, between you and I, I must show her up this weekend. I simply must. Were you at the Kitridge Party last week? Oh, I doubt that you were! It was a select crowd...."

You bitch.

"Mrs. Dandry," *she* continues, "arrives impeccably in style. She always has been the utmost in style. I only hope when I'm that age that I can still manage to carry myself through society that well."

Mrs. Dandry is 44. She hardly needs any help carrying herself.

"Mrs. Dandry steals the show, just gets gasp after gasp when she walks in. She's wearing this fur...This gorgeous fur. It was smokey and blueish and just pulled the hues off her diamonds wonderfully! So, I had to ask her ALL about it. It was a one of a kind, especially made for her. *Snow Ermine*, she called it. I simply must show her up one for that! She was the talk of the party all evening!"

Snow Ermine???

"I do so hope I get to see your little place this weekend. I plan to come, unless, of course, something else pops up."

"Its a grand place," says he to *she*, "with oaks so big they must have been there for hundreds of years. And they're the good kind of oaks. Weathered oaks...I think they call them live oaks....yes, that's it....Water oaks fail you and fall. There are no water oaks there. But, then again, I'm going on what others have told me. I wouldn't know a water oak if it fell on me! And there's a creek-"

"Oh, look! Its Eve!" screams *she* patting me and he on the

back before taking leave for "better people" on this street ....and you could even see it in her face as *she* fled from my friend and me....Eve who was with Steve turned to see *she* screaming, "Eve!" and tried to turn onto Green Street. (Interesting. I had never thought Eve, who was with Steve, better people than me).

To have been subtle would have been something short of a lie, considering what history my friend and I have. So I smacked him on the arm the moment *she* was gone.

"Why, oh WHY tell me WHY did you invite (*she*)."

"Oh, *she's* harmless."

"ARE YOU KIDDING ME!"

"I sort of feel bad for her. I mean, look at her."

There was *she* trying to keep up with Eve and Steve who were trying to escape onto Green Street.

And my friend, being the compassionate man he is, says simply, "*She* has no one. You see? Besides....doesn't *she* look hungry? *She* can't be eating! So thin!"

And that was how *she* ended up at the party. *She* had arrived just some moments before dinner, whilst I, my friend, and Mr. and Mrs. Dandry were having cocktails. Mr. and Mrs. Dandry were continuing an argument about the poor, one they had read of in a novel. They argued about "Howard's End," by E.M. Forster.

"He's so right," says Mrs. Dandry, "You give the poor the same lifestyle we're accustomed to and it will inspire him!"

79

"Darling, you're off on that one. Forster meant to suggest that you give him money. You let him decide what he wants to do with it."

She walks in, boldly moving into the room and into their conversation with the utmost in rudeness. "I read that same book and one line put it best when it comes to the poor. It's something like, 'the poor should only be approached by the poet or the statistician.' Who cares about the poor, I certainly don't....."

I was standing with my back to her, rolling my eyes, trying to put on my better-than-pleased face before I spun around to greet her. My friend was to my right and I noticed a strange-eyed fright beginning to dull the shine in his light eyes. Slowly I could see a grimace form, where once the most angelic smile could repel all sin. I'd never seen such a mad man's gaze before, and don't care to again, especially from my friend. But, so transfixed was I on what *she* was saying about her dislike and nonchalance for the poor that I did not notice, nor did it even dawn on me, what everyone else was suddenly so shocked by. Mrs. Dandry was clutching with slow gasps at her heart, her chest...and Mr. Dandry lowered and shook his head with some disbelief.

She noticed the reaction from Mr. and Mrs. Dandry and persisted with, "Well....What do you think? Isn't it divine?"

Now I took notice too, even took notice of Mrs. Dandry's repulsion.

STORIES INSPIRED BY **SIOUXSIE**

"I guess I got one up on you again, Mrs. Dandry! Your coat is beautiful, I agree. Oh, look at you all! Look at you! I knew you'd be amazed at my stole, but I never assumed you would be so awestruck!"

"I don't think I follow you, woman. How do you think you got one up on me? What on earth are you talking about?" Asked Mrs. Dandry with this bothered sense of displeasure.

"Your fur, from the Kitridge party! The Snow Ermine you had specially made for you. I agree it is divine, but this," *she* said rubbing the stole, "this is a masterpiece."

"*Snow* Ermine? *Snow* Ermine?"

"Yes! That adorable coat you had last weekend! Don't tell me you've forgotten already."

"*FAUX* ERMINE.....not SNOW! It was faux! A FAKE!"

And poor *she* looked so suddenly puzzled at Mrs. Dandry. "I can't believe you would admit to wearing a fake."

So to clarify, convinced that *she* was as stupid as we had always said *she* was, Mrs. Dandry again simplified the statement for her. "It was a fake, woman. A fake! How dare you show up here wearing such a thing! I hope to God, for your sake, that pelt isn't the animal I think it to be."

"Fox! I had a hunter come and round them up."

"Oh, dear God," said Mrs. Dandry with a simple shake, nearly unable to stand, the heels in which she stood teetering

81

unstable, nearly sending her reeling to the floor. "Where did you get the stole???? HOW did you get the stole?" Mrs. Dandry didn't dare stare at my friend. The simple twitch turned to mad-eyed would have broken the hardest of hearts.

"The furrier in Savannah! He's owed me a favor or two for some time! Bastardly little foxes didn't cost me a penny! I came out here to see just how small and cozy this place was. I mean....what's the word I'm looking for? I wanted to make sure it wasn't too rustic. Well, as I was walking around I saw all of these foxes running about everywhere! Then it occurred to me! I could have a one of a kind fox stole. But that's not the best of it. He's working on a full length coat as we speak. But, I simply had to have something for this weekend. And look how nicely they shine! The furrier says they must have been eating RATHER well," Said *she* to my friend turning to see him leaning with broken gaze at the wall. "So you'd better be careful! They were probably eating whatever you were throwing out! Probably digging through the trash, the nasty little things!"

She only paused for a moment inquisitively. "Are you alright?" My friend looked frightful, and *she* asking him was guarantee that even the most self centered, egotistical of maniacs could see that he had gone quickly from frightened, to sad, to mad, to finally dangerous. Said *she* stupidly, "You look as though you should have a drink!"

He said nothing, moved slowly away from the wall, never

removing his eyes once from the fox stole about her neck and moved to her with the steady stroll of a man about to murder.

"Yes it is a fine stole...." That tone in his droning guttural throat was unlike anything I recall having been uttered from his tongue. He lifted his hand and began to pat the damned, dead things that had once been his beloved companions. But, the petting was a speed that bordered on a dream.

"A fine coat these foxes had, I agree." Oh, his voice sounded pained already. *She* smiled, while he slowly turned his cheek up to her face, a tear trail dripping sadly as he leaned in closer to whisper, "A fine coat....indeed. How clever of you to have killed these things, skinned them and find a furrier that meets your needs."

He now had both hands patting the stole on either side of her neck. The speed increased. "How lucky I am," said he to *she*, "that you should have saved me from these foxy fiends!" And now he was hitting at her chest as *she* tried to pull away. Alas, to no avail. His right hand grabbed the stole and his left hand grabbed her long straw-like, thin, blond hair as *she* screamed. *She* had the misfortune of looking to me, who could comfort her none. I turned my eyes to the fire for a moment, did not dare afford *she* my sympathy.

"Mrs. Dandry!!! PLEASE! Mrs. DANDRY! He's GONE INSANE! HE'S HURTING ME!"

And Mrs. Dandry? She had long since gone to fix a drink. All Mrs. Dandry could truly hear was *she* beginning to scream. The rest of us saw the most gruesome image occurring quickly in that quaint parlor now tainted with the hideous display of cruelty....not on his part mind you, but on *she's*.

We saw my friend having *she* brought to her knees. Her own hands turned to claws as *she* tried to free herself with one hand of the clinched grip of hair my friend pulled grimly from her head. Her other hand tried to scratch the man's eyes out. But anger in its purist form, the visions in his own head of seeing his beloved foxes hunted, murdered and now worn before him was a pain much more unbearable. Her scratches into him were simply nothing more than a nuisance.

She screamed and oh, God, how *she* did scream! Blood was beginning to spill from her forehead and the hair on her small head was slowly ripped and torn from its roots. And as the blood began to stream past her own eyes, causing the whole episode from her view to grow red, *she* fell to the floor having fainted.

None of us questioned her misery. And my friend, once she had grown limp in his grip, did not cease to pull and pull and pull the hair from her head. Not I, not the Dandrys, not a one of us ever said with a simple human instinct, "Stop." Not once. We watched him go down on her, pull now with both hands every last hair from her head, his face resting against the hides he had once loved with every fiber of his angelic smile. His grip only letting up softly to pat the things here and there with bloody hand, saying through screams

STORIES INSPIRED BY SIOUXSIE

and tearful streams, "My babies....my little babies."

My friend left *she* there to bleed, pulling the stole from around her neck and hugging it tightly against his breast as the Dandrys and I went to console him.

She stayed there for some time, incoherent even when we finally picked her up and placed her outside on the doorstep. My friend went to bed, as the Dandrys took leave. There was to be no celebration this weekend. There was to be no love, no life, and no pursuit of the beauty we find pleasing in humanity, nor in nature. I stayed behind to hold my friend.

We shall take a darker turn in our story now. For as polite as I may have been throughout the preceding script I have no choice but to honestly cringe when I begin to think of the regret many of us at that weekend getaway call upon when asked about the scalping of *she*. Not one of us will regret the action itself, for the devilish *she* needed it, deserved every hair pulled from her head. What we all regret is that moment days before near Green Street. You recall, correct? When *she* approached my friend and me, intruding herself upon us, inviting herself with ill mannered style to our weekend retreat? Yes, that's the moment we all regret. And none of us blame my friend for his actions, for having the hide of her head pulled back from its skin. None of us blame him for that at all. We all blame him for being kind, and caring of *she*, naive that *she*, as evil as a thing as *she* could be, for not killing her off completely. And *that*, to this very day, is the thing that we all recall and regret, what we all find fault in. That he let the woman live and let be....

She is not seen these days, you see. Aside from her physical grotesqueness enough to have bruised her ego to the point of seclusion, the little sympathy *she* received when people heard of what *she* had done was enough to send her into total silence. *She* never pressed charges against my friend. I doubt *she* had the nerve. And in our strange little circle of social elitism, when the story of *she* and the foxes is told none of our names are included. It is simply told like such, "Someone pulled the very hair from her head in retaliation."

Of course, there are moments when you do see *she* and of these moments I speak metaphorically. Any one of us can be at a party and see someone who is new in our ranks behaving with frightful rudeness. As a matter of fact, I was at a cocktail party not more than three days ago when I saw a woman who reminded me of *she*. Like *she*, this new girl looked of bone and loose skin, eating one slice of cucumber cut into quarters for her meal.

"I can't have anything more," said the *new she*, "or I'll get FAT! God! Don't you just hate FAT people??? The only people I hate more are the poor...Why should they work? They live off our money anyway! MY taxes!"

I could only summon a subtle smile, nothing more than a cocked grin, nothing revealing the brilliance of an immediate emotion, but rather, the reminiscence of what had happened to the previous *she*...My eyes didn't leave this *new she*, this rancid girl who rambled on with an arrogant and plastic purpose. Some around her chuckled and some knowing the demise of the previous *she* looked to me for a lead.

I did nothing at first, but seethed at how we with money and we of a privileged breed tend to think of ourselves beaming with superiority. The whole time the *new she* shrieked and carried on with her morbid interests (those interests of self and of stature), I could do nothing but stare. From the corner of her eyes the *new she* could see me, and her eyes would dart away quickly. I think, perhaps my eyes were the only thing at all visible to anyone in the room. They were piercing.

"Excuse me." Asked the *new she*, "Is there something wrong?"

"I beg your pardon?"

"Well, its rather rude, if you ask me."

"Do come again...What's rude?"

"You are STARING at me."

"I do apologize. You're absolutely right....Well, somewhat right...I've been admiring your coat."

And her eyes went alight with the self congratulatory promise that someone had noticed the luxurious and expensive pelt....Yes, the *new she* had been validated by her clothes. The *new she* suddenly modeled it for me, opening it up to show the organza lining, rubbing the sleeves, feeling the softness mother nature had intended for its original wearer. The nerve of her....The *new she* wrapped her own arms around herself, hugging herself.

"Isn't it divine???"

"In a matter of speaking, yes...All things made from God are divine."

"God took extra time making this little devil, just so I could one day wear it."

I went slowly to her with the hand outstretched as if to touch it. Off in the corner of the room, by some anonymous man who knew me and my attachment to the story of *she*, I heard a voice force clear its throat. Do you think for a moment that it might have stopped me? That it might have halted me into rationality? Heavens, no. I saw a nemesis before me, covered in the skin of a helpless being having died for this bitch of a woman's vanity.

As humans we're lucky, we can choose our heroic moments where death, when chosen, can be made in moments of grand valor. But what rested on this woman's back were the tears and pain of a creature who could not understand that its life had been intended from its inception to belong to *ANY she*, to live so that it may die and make *ANY she* look better, for heaven knows these women can't do it of their own free will, not with their boney faces, not with their scrawny frames, not even with their monstrous personalities.

My subtle hand felt the pelt and a silence swept the room, devouring even the most entranced of party goers. With but a whisper I questioned, "Is it....fox?"

"Oh, heavens, no! Simply rabbit."

"Simply rabbit, you say?"

"Yes. I adore fox, though, don't you? But, only real foxes, you know. Not the fake ones. So many people opt for faux and I'm simply abhorred by fake anything."

"Is that so?" Said I with such a smile that lent a twist to sinister. I spun around to the pressing crowd and uttered, "Did everyone hear that? Only REAL foxes, the *new she* said! No faux foxes for the *new she*." And from the crowd you could hear the sound of muttered chuckles and broken snickering. This *new she*? What did she attempt to do? *New she* looked on with happiness, of course, for the *new she* was the sort that adored the attention paid to her coat, the sort of person who cannot exist unless this *new she* is persistently given attention.

God, the room chilled then, that same silence mentioned before sending a creep through the parlor room that only punctuated what I had to say next to the *new she*.

"I have a friend with some lovely property out in the country." I held her hand in mine, as if to elude to some sincerity. All partying eyes around me sparked alive. "Please say you'll join us one weekend??? We can hunt you down some real foxes...."

"Oh, I'D LOVE TO!"

And a roar and an applause erupted from everyone.

CHEAP RED AND NEARLY DEAD

FOR PENI....FOR OLD TIME'S SAKE

GREGORY PATRICK

Best friends can be bound by a myriad of things that only they two hold true. Some find it to be a sporting event that keeps them calling one another, and others find it events in the park, shopping sprees, or delirious evenings club hopping. But, these two had a wine fancy that glued them tightly to each other's side for the better part of some decade.

Don't get any pretentious ideas about them sipping wine from long stems, enjoying its bouquets with cheeses, or even of societies built around barrels and crates that waited to be tasted then jettisoned to a spittoon. Only know these two spent their time *guzzling* wine, cracking bottle after bottle to see just which hue of red gave a better buzz and of which shiraz made you happy and which made you mad. On occasion they would dress for their drinking, but most of the time their wine tasted best in casual gear; blue jeans, or even in their pajamas if it was late enough in the evening, and once I remember stopping by to see them by the pool that they shared, each with a bottle, each with nothing more than a towel and a big smile wrapped around them. Their lips and teeth had an overcast of purple, the sun pushing forth their euphorias even more. And what can one do? You just sigh, nod, maybe try to smile....then say as I had done that day, "I'll catch you two some other time."

The friendship began at a party for the Academy Awards. Now, I recall hearing stories about some distaste they had for each other prior to that night, but as in all great romances it was a shared interest that finally allowed the flood gates to reveal others similar needs.

At that particular party (had you gone to every corner of the kitchen to explore) you would have found beer here and whiskey there, but not a drop of wine to be found. That's what pressed Meredith into depression. It made the party dull, boring. Beer is boring, or so says she. And as people mingled, cackling and laughing with dreary whiskey induced slurring, she couldn't help but notice "that scrawny, red headed man" in the corner drinking from a paper bag. Now, that clue alone wouldn't suggest anything remarkable, you know. It could have been Jack Daniel's, a bottle of vodka he had brought all his own...it could even have been a fifth of a liquor flavored like chocolate or coffee, the kind of which Meredith abhorred. But, she studied him from the kitchen for a while, wondering just what was that in that bag? He would lift and swig, head held back and gulped. And just then did she see it, so sweet it slipped between his lips, the light reflecting from it as it slowly dribbled to his chin, his hand as in a motion made for romantic

94

movies, slowly lifting to catch it lest it fall upon his white shirt. The shirt! Seems there had been one or two drops he had neglected to fetch, for their spotted on occasion were the subtle signs of red wine having polka dotted his attire.

It was as if all the commotion and roar of that party's swing suddenly went silent as the subtle smile came across Meredith's face. Wine.....WINE!

"That's what I want, that's what would make me happy."

So, all party goers ceased to be and slowly she stepped towards Eric, eyes transfixed on the paper bag...

As was his action from the moment he arrived at the party to the moment known as now, Eric with head held back gobbled down some grand gulp of his drink, spotting from the corner of his eye that woman coming at him.

"What are-," he had to wipe his chin again, "What are you doing here?"

"Looking for a drink."

"There's a faucet over where you were."

"What have you got? What is that? Merlot? Cab? Valpollicello?"

"Val's pole of *what?*"

"Valpollicello."

He only arched his brow.

"I know you've got wine, Eric."

95

"What's it to you, crazy lady?"

"Listen, you'll give me a glass or I'll spill the beans. Got it?"

"What do I care if you tell someone I've got wine?"

"I'm not stupid, Eric. You're afraid to be seen with wine."

"Oh, bullshit."

"Why the paper bag?"

He fell short of an answer.

"This crowd isn't likely to find a wine drinker very....masculine, I think. Hmmm??? This may be an Academy Awards party, but the intellect ends there. This is an excuse to drink and you know it."

"It is not. Jack believes in the arts." He was referring to me. I'm Jack and I could care less for the arts.

"Jack could care less for the arts. This is just another one of his excuses to throw a party. Like Columbus Day...President's Day...." And Grandparents Day. It is a holiday. I swear it is. Check your calendar. "And don't forget....what was that? Boxing day? I saw you at that party and don't deny it."

"Don't be so smug, lady. I remember you bringing that hideous girl with you to the Flag Day Party. And if that's not enough, I even remember seeing you lose your lunch at the Just-Cause-Its-Tuesday Party. So, you like to drink, too. I know you do, and don't deny it."

"I'm not denying it.'

"Then where's your drink?"

"There's no wine."

He smiles, that arrogant, *'ha ha, I gotcha'* grin and slyly whispers, "That's why I bring my own."

"I don't understand. Why wouldn't Jack have wine? He's had wine before."

"Yes, and he decided to stop having wine at his parties cause Jack says only you, yes that's right only YOU drink it then act like a fool around everyone else." Meredith had a tendency to behave in ways that the rest of us happy with whiskey and beer couldn't tolerate. Every libation has its own euphoric reaction on the personality. Beer makes you everyone's friend and liquor can make you sedated or a tyrannical, depending on the person. (It makes Eric a fascist and that's more than likely why you'll find him drinking wine which leads me to-) wine makes you either stupid giddy or sensual and only your genetic disposition will decide. I had found that through the many of the parties I have thrown that wine makes both Eric and Meredith stupid giddy....

"Oh. Come on, share with me, Eric!" And she pauses to consider exactly what she could offer.... "I'll make it worth your while."

"I'm gay, Meredith."

"That's not what I meant. I've got a great bottle of Bordeaux I could share with you at a later date."

"Let me get this straight.... You'll gladly pay me Tuesday for a hamburger today?"

"Quoting *Popeye* doesn't exactly impress people."

"What year?"

"'88."

"1888?"

"Oh, good grief! 1988, you heathen."

"Not bad....but, not good enough. I want the whole bottle."

"Well, that depends. What are you hiding in that brown paper bag."

"You taste and tell me."

"Really?"

"Yes...but, you have to agree to give me the entire bottle of the Bordeaux before hand."

"Eric!"

"No deal!"

"Fine. You win. It's insane what I'll do for a drink."

"I knew you'd see it my way. Now fetch a glass."

"Forget the damned glass, just give me the bottle."

Meredith's hands grasped around the brown paper bag as though it were water deep within the well of a worn desert. Meredith gulped a heavy enough bit to set her self satisfied.

"Oh, Eric, that's good." Her eyes all alight with pleasure. "That's real good. Yummy."

"I know. Worth trading the Bordeaux for?"

She thinks for a moment smacking her lips. "Yes, I think so. What is it anyway?"

"Here. Take another sip."

She attempts to guess at its brilliance. "Chateau Monmot 1987?"

"Eh, no."

"Vandenberg, '89?"

"Lord, I thought you were better at wine tasting than this! No, its not Vandenberg. Sounds like some kinda car, actually."

"Well, what is it, then?"

"Oh, one of my absolute favorites," he says pulling the bottle from the brown paper back. "Yellow Dog!!! Woo-hoo!"

Meredith's jaw drops as her eyes zone in quickly to the brilliant white price tag proudly announcing the cost at $3.99 a bottle.

"Are you shitting me? Yellow Dog? I traded a bottle of Bordeaux for a sip of....Yellow DOG????"

"Hey, that was no sip, babe. That was a definite chug if I ever saw one. Let this be a lesson to you! Cheap reds rock! All that pretentious Vandenburgen, Hoofenschmergen, Macrommont crap! You people don't know good wine until you taste it! And you tasted it and boy, were you fooled! You see? All you people and your labels! I could have smacked on some dorky Hoffschneider

99

1987 name on here and charged you $30 and you would never have known!"

She laughs! Can you imagine that? She laughs? "You are evil, Eric. Just....evil. I'm gonna get my fair trades worth. Hand that bottle here."

A friendship corked from cheap red wine. How divine...The two were inseparable from that moment forth. Cheap red wine was made for best friends. Pretentiousness and pomposity brim over in high priced Merlot and Bordeaux, but cheap red cabernets were made for the days two friends do nothing but sit and laugh. Meredith would do her best to impress upon Eric some crazy named vineyards.

"Boulet-vous who? Chakaraka what? Zitzenfurben???? Come on, Meredith! Yellow Dog!"

"That's it. From now on I'm calling you 'Cheap Red.'"

I recall fondly that decade best. If you saw Eric, then Meredith was just around the corner...and if you saw Meredith, then you knew Eric was near the restroom somewhere. They were at every party, you know, and when they did arrive it was if they had their own language, their own sense of purpose and allowed everyone in on the fun. They were the entertainment du'jour for the better more of 10 full years. To some they were offensive, to others, brilliantly wicked.

They never made apology nor remorse of any kind for the

100

way they were. As a matter of fact, they thrived on their eccentricities, and all under the guise of red wine. Not to mention you would find them in some of the most enthralling situations.

I recall a trip I took to the supermarket. I was there for some simple things, bread, milk cheese, and who do you think I should see, but Eric standing near the aisle that had an extensive selection of Brie.

"Eric! Hello! How do you do?"

"Hey! Doing good, what about you?"

"I'm well. No Meredith?"

"Oh, she's here, over by the pate~."

"Found a wine yet?"

"You know Meredith. I let her pick it out. If it were me we'd go for cheap."

"What did she get?"

"God, something I can't pronounce, something from France. Twenty bucks a bottle! You know, I think someone lied to her."

"Oh, really!"

"Yeah! I've found some great $7 dollar bottles in my time. And who says the best reds come from France? That's a lie. The best one's are from Chile."

"You think?"

"Sure! Meredith always has to look her best, though, always has to impress, always has to show off....Oh, here she is now."

And what did my eyes spy, but the exquisite girl painted from head to toe stark gray. If you need to back up and read that sentence once more, I would not blame you. I confess to you the woman was painted gray. Her hair had been painted black, as had been done with her lips and eyes. Her clothes? Some strange concoction of mismatched purple sweats!

I was stunned. I took a step back to inspect the spectacle that I was sure to be a stroke of some sort coming on. But, no...It was a legitimate vision, it was a real scene. She was painted gray alright, and behaved as though not a thing were out of place.

"Meredith?"

"Well, hi, Jack! Got the red wine! And the pate~! Eric, have you picked out a brie, yet?"

"What do you think of this one?"

"It's....well....I guess for what we have to select from it will have to do."

"Meredith?" I piped in again.

"Yes?"

"Is everything...Wait," I stopped to question the intention, the reason. Why would she be dressed in such a mess and painted gray....GRAY! They were obviously already drunk. "You two have been drinking already, haven't you! What is this? Bottle three or something?"

They both looked somewhat confused and even had the

nerve to look at me as if I were off my rocker....I wasn't the one painted gray!

"Well, no...Haven't had a drop yet today," says Meredith. "That's why we're somewhat in a hurry. We're anxious to get started."

"Are you feeling ok?" Eric asked of me, even putting his hands on my shoulder to offer comfort for whatever might be ailing me....ME!

Stunned, I paused for a moment before blurting quite loudly, "I'm fine! It's Meredith I'm worried about!"

"Why, what have you heard?"

"HEARD???? It's what I see!!! Meredith! You're painted gray! GRAY, I SAY! GRAY!"

She rolls here eyes at me, can you believe it? Rolls her eyes.

"No, I'm not.....I'm painted puce....a shade of lavender-"

"I know what puce is, that's not my concern. Why are you painted that way!"

"We've been cast in a play!"

"I beg your pardon?"

"Oh, when was it Eric?" She asks him tapping her toe.

"I think about three weeks ago?"

"Has it been that long?"

"Yeah."

"Well, three weeks ago.....Sunday, right?"

"Yes, on a Sunday."

"We go for Sushi and saki..."

"*Shaki....,*" Says Eric mimicking being drunk.

"And we get a little fumbled by the saki, you know. We can have our fill of wine, but saki will getcha! Anyway, We were bored! Sunday, buzzed in the middle of the afternoon and bored! We wander out of the sushi house, stumbling down the street when we pass the theatre and they're holding auditions."

"You didn't!" I screamed.

"WE DID! We auditioned, blitzed off our asses."

Eric chimes in with, "We got cast!"

"We're doing Blithe Spirit!"

"I got cast as the lead! Charles Condomine!"

"And I'm his first dead wife come back to haunt him. We're on our way there now to do a Sunday matinee."

"Blah....Sunday theatre is filled with nothing but old people....OH! You'll match all the hair out in the audience Meredith!" They had begun to speak to each other, leaving me there in the supermarket a somewhat slight bit embarrassed that I was being seen with the two of them. So I ask Meredith, "Well, why don't you put the gray-"

"Puce."

"Why not put the puce make up on at the theatre?"

"Oh!!!! Well," She leans in to see if she can make it sound

104

somewhat sneaky. "We want to see if we'll end up in *The Enquirer.* *'Puce woman seen in Publix. Mother of Batboy?'* Don't you see?"

"Batboy?"

"Take one good look at Eric. Those ears? He could pass for an over dramatized sighting of batboy."

"It's true. I could." He says.

I stupidly ask who 'Batboy' was.

Meredith gives me quick insight into tabloid journalism and all its varied characters. "You never read *The Star? The Enquirer?* Batboy is a legend, Jack. He's just brilliant."

"Brilliant." Eric's tone made it sound as though they were quietly honoring an icon. "Especially when they spotted him driving that car, remember?"

"God, yes!!! He's got this wormy face and these teeth!" And again they had begun their own conversation of which only those two participated.

"The teeth!"

"These teeth that are like all gnarled and fangy....And no hair! Just like Eric! Ha Ha!"

"On his head, she means, not on his teeth."

"No, not on the teeth."

"We've really got to be going if we're gonna make it to the theatre."

"Shit! We'll be late! See you later, Jack!"

And in the moments it took for them to pursue their strange charades in public I could do nothing but stand silent and watch them carry on. As they moved towards the checkout, the looks they garnered were impressive, inquisitive. Instead of feeling embarrassed, as I first had, I began to feel uniquely proud of them and of the courage that they often summoned to simply just be who they are and nothing more.

I did see the play mind you, and the two of them were incredibly gifted as actors. Never would I have thought in a million years their portrayal of satyrical characters of the Noel Coward sort would have been so perfect....And it was true. Meredith's make up matched every head of hair in the audience that Sunday. I was so driven with their performance and the manner in which the casting had been landed that I invited them to sushi once the show was over.

"Come on, you're performances were unbelievable and if I recall, you two have a tradition on Sundays. I'm taking you for sushi and saki."

"*Shaki*," Eric reminds me with a smile.

"Yes. Excellent performance. We'll catch a little buzz before you two head home to enjoy that bottle of wine."

"What bottle?" Eric asks. "Meredith, are you holding out on me? What bottle?"

Meredith looks to me puzzled. "I'm not sure I understand. What bottle of wine, Jack?"

106

"The one you bought this afternoon."

"*That* bottle? You're gonna have to keep up. Oh, Lord, that's long gone!"

"When?"

Eric confesses quickly it was done somewhere around act two. But, Meredith corrects him. "No, third act, when the portly girl playing your LIVING wife was running into the set!"

"Jack, did you see that? That was hilarious!"

The poor girl cast to play Eric's current wife in the production was sadly enough on the heavy side, something the set designers hadn't taken into consideration when they determined how secure some of the props should be. And as the heavy girl made some attempt to run screaming off stage through a painted scene of trees and bushes managed to catch her hip along side the frame and knocked the entire facade to the ground. Exposing technicians, and nearly nude actors waiting in the wings.

"That was just about the time I was trying to finish the bottle off. I was due back on set, you know."

"Meredith, may I ask? Are you going to the restaurant painted puce?"

"Well, of course!" She says patting Eric on the head, "Come on, Cheap Red! We need more Batboy sightings!"

And in some manner of foreboding Eric says, "I'll have to find you a nickname, Meredith."

The entire evening moved rather well, and considering the graciousness of the restaurant's staff it appeared as though there were nothing particular about Meredith painted head to toe with stage make up. But, I must make mention of some peculiarity, of course, for no interjection of Meredith and Eric would be complete without one.

We were forced to sit at the sushi bar, for the extent of the restaurant was packed to capacity. The bar itself was a sort of 'L' shape, with me at the corner and Eric to my right, Meredith to my left. All was perfectly lovely and dinner was enjoyed in the fashion in which it was intended....until Eric decided to make a toast.

"Ok. ok. ok...." Poor boy was already drunk. "I would like....(burp)... to *take* this opportunity to...*take* a moment and...and to...*take* a reflect on what a great day it's been, you know. I *take* it, you all agree. And don't...*take* it for granted. *Take* it for what it is.... The weather was brilliant. Our performance was ingenious. Did you hear me? *Ingenious.* The set has to be repaired giving the union workers something to do to keep them employed for yet another week, which is good. And I'm here sitting with my friends while some fat girl cast in a play is at home crying because one swift turn of her hip is enough to knock down shrubbery......I adore you both. Thank you, thank deeply for a perfect evening."

Now, he taps my glass with his in a perfect toast, but since Meredith is too far from him to actually, physically touch, he yells to her as loud as he possibly can, while motioning a toast, "Chink!"

Of course, you and I both know he was mimicking the sound of the two glasses hitting each other in toast. Slowly, though, a stillness creeps through the sushi house...and Eric's eyes grow wide, the restaurant staff stops in their tracks, all patrons stop eating and look our direction, and the man preparing the sushi, slicing eel, slices even louder, with conviction, with a taint of anger in his motion.

Meredith lowers her head and tries not to chuckle. Eric peels back into his chair, grabbing at his chest.

"Oh, my GOD! NO! Oh, MY GOD! NO! THAT'S NOT WHAT I MEANT!!!!"

I tired my best to console him. "I doubt anyone heard you, Eric."

"Are you kidding me! I just screamed CHINK in a restaurant full of Orientals!"

And again, that steady silence got colder.

"Asians!" I screamed, "Asians, Asians, Asians! Calling them Orientals is rude! Rugs are oriental! FOOD is oriental! But, people are ASIANS!"

"Oh, God, I fucked up! We'd better go! God, I can't BELIEVE I just did that!"

"Check, please!"

Needless to say, the service was terrible after that.

And for nearly ten good solid years, that's what life was like with Eric and Meredith around. Then something shifted as destiny loves to do. I noticed that Eric and Meredith were not to be found as often. They did not come to the parties anymore, they weren't seen around town, and the stories about their mad adventures were heard less and less. I was not the only one who noticed, their definite disappearance had many more than just concerned.....they were bored. The uniqueness in their friendship was something that everyone who knew them was envious of; a friendship that defied common definition. It was if they were perfectly suited for one another, but ill equipped for romance. Had they both been heterosexual, or homosexual for that matter, they would have been the romance that is remembered in literature for years to come. And whose to say their connection wasn't a sort of romance? Whose to say that love and coupling have everything to do with the genetic make up we're given at birth? And furthermore, whose to say that even though there was no sexual stimulation between them that what they had wasn't a love more powerful than any husband and wife could have ever achieved?

We soon discovered the reason for the absence. Meredith had taken ill, seriously ill and had been in the hospital for some time. Unfortunately, her prognosis was terminal and she was not expected to live for too much longer. Eric was at her side day and night, even going so far as to pull in a cot to the hospital room where Meredith was so he could sleep there.

Just because of the nature in their speech with one another, they treated the whole episode on rather comical terms, never once pulling darkness into the dismal situation. Each morning he would wake, wash his face, run down to grab a coffee from the vending machine, then return to his best friend to ask while tugging at her leg, "Hey.....Hey.....Are you dead yet?"

Groggily she would answer, "No, but *you* will be soon if you don't let me sleep."

"Listen, if you're gonna be dead soon, why don't you get up! I mean, you'll be sleeping an awful lot once they throw you in the ground."

"God, I feel awful....How much did we drink last night."

Eric laughs and says, "We didn't drink anything, sleepyhead. Its the morphine...."

"Oh...yeah....I nearly forgot."

"So how long do you think it will be?"

"For what?"

"Before you're gone."

"Well, I hope its any day now. I mean, if its gonna happen then let's just get it over with. I HATE being in this bed, in this hospital.....in this outfit for God's sake."

"Tell me about it...You've been *nearly* dead forever now...." And his eye twinkled and he brightly shined a stunning brilliance in his smile. "That's it! That's your nickname! 'Nearly Dead!'"

111

Meredith laughed at him for as long as she could before the coughing was too unbearable to ignore. It was becoming more and more obvious that their time together was dwindling.

"Yeah.....Nearly Dead." As much as they had tried these few weeks to keep their spirits high, it was the natural course of things to feel a sadness dawning. Now, this had nothing to do with death itself, for they had discussed that on many occasions throughout their ten year run. They believed that death was not the end, but just another journey the soul is bound to take. The sadness they were beginning to experience was the fear of loneliness. They were to be parted and split and not a day had gone by in the last ten years where such a thing had happened.

Meredith had already begun to pressure Eric into leaving the hospital on occasion, to go out and get some fresh air. The worse Meredith got, the more she persisted.

"Go! Have fun! Do something! Your sitting around here all day like some buzzard is depressing me."

"Nah, I'm fine. And I prefer 'vulture,' thank you. It has a more sinister tone to it."

Secretly she praised him for standing by her side. She feared the loneliness, too. She feared being alone when death may come, and feared Eric being sent back into the world without her.

By now the illness had taken so much out of her, that one sordid morning the doctor in care of Meredith pulled Eric aside to suggest plans be made for her burial. "I don't expect her to be with us tomorrow morning," said the doctor with as much politeness and respect that he could summon.

Eric only stood in the hallway, staring with a transfixed denial on the floor. If he moved, he thought, he could cry. There staring he stayed for an hour or more before composing his reasoning and rationality and returning to Meredith's room with his morning coffee.

"Still dying, darling?"

"God, worse than that.....I'm so friggin loopy. How much morphine did I do last night?"

"You did soooo much that they've had to have another semi of it trucked in. And you know, I told the doctor, 'Just give her a couple of bottles of red wine.....That'll sock her out.' I've seen you pass out before and its not pretty...."

"Mmmmm, that sounds so good. Red Wine. A Beaujolais....a good one."

There was a look in his eye that revealed precisely what he was so hoping to hide. But, Eric had never been good at that. He could forever hide his emotions from the tongue, never once speak about what hurt him. What angered him? Surely, he was forever ready to spit profanity at whatever it was that annoyed him, but not with matters of the heart. That was impossible. Never would he say he was hurt. He didn't have to. Those eyes of his would get big, would swell, would dart away, and when the pain was so great it was overwhelming him, he looked the part of 6 year old nearly about to pout.

Meredith pipes up, realizing with some grand determination that this may be it....This may be their last day together. "I have an idea," she says. She motions for him to come closer.

"Hey, Nearly Dead, I'm not to sure about that breath of yours."

"Oh, get over here!"

He leans in closer pretending to make this face of repulsion, trying to find the humor always in this upsetting scenery.

"I have an idea," she says in sneaky whisper. "Why don't *you* go out and grab *me* a bottle of that Beaujolais that I like." She turns her head left and right to see if anyone is listening. "Bring it back here with some glasses and let's do this dying thing right."

He smiles slightly, a slant in his eyes calling about some mischief. "What if we get caught?"

"What are they gonna do? *Kill* me? Kick me out of the hospital? Go! Hurry back! I'm nearly dead!"

"You can say that again."

Within an hour's time he had returned with a backpack and how the nurses did not realize that he was carrying something suspicious is beyond anyone's guess. He had a ball cap on, the brim pulled so tightly down to conceal his face he gave the impression he was hiding something. And the backpack itself clanged and clinked from the bottles of wine hitting up against one another.

"How many did you bring?" Meredith asked so pleased.

"Three!"

"NO!"

"YES!"

He pulls out from the backpack the Beaujolais and only showed it to Meredith who had anxious hands outstretched to greet it.

"Nope," defies Eric, "We'll get to that shortly. First.....Yellow Dog!"

"NO!"

"YES! One for you," handing the cheap bottle to Meredith, "and one for me."

"You just couldn't resist, could you?"

"They don't call me Cheap Red for nothing. Besides, cheap red wine was designed with best friends in mind. Your Beaujolais was made for pretentiousness and special occasions."

Halfway through each of their respective bottles the effects of the wine had begun to show on their purple grins. They were laughing at the giddiest of things and reminiscing about some of the strange characters they had encountered throughout their days.

"Remember the homeless woman? Toada?" So called because she resembled....well, a toad. "Always suing the government? Her lawyer was her imaginary friend."

"How fucked up is that! And she was paying him!"

"He doesn't come close, though, to when we were actors. What was that crazy security guy's name?"

"Big old' Bill! Kept telling you, 'Eric....I don't mind if you're gay or straight. Won't mean shit when the aliens come.' The look on your face when he said that was priceless, Eric! 'The aliens?' You asked. 'As in Mexicans?' Jesus, I thought I was gonna lose it."

"The funny thing is, people think you and I are weird. They don't know half the people we've seen that really take the cake. Like the guy in Melbourne."

"Melbourne is full of whacks. You'll have to be more specific."

"You and I were walking down that weird little street that had an art gallery....And there was that painting of the old man, straw hat, overalls, hands in pocket, just a grinning! We sat there for the longest time thinking, 'How unusual a painting. It's so.....*unusual.*' He looked like some serial killer. We snap back to reality, come out of our daze, spin around to leave and the man is standing right there! Straw hat, overalls, hands in pocket-"

"Just grinning! I have never screamed so loud in my life! My favorite, though is Carlos."

"Carlos? I don't remember any Carlos"

"Eric, come on! From the vending machine!"

"Oh, yeah!"

Meredith tosses out the thickest Latin accent she can muster, "Hey, Enrico.....Joo Lik-a hot penis???"

"I was like, 'Beg your pardon?'"

"And again he asks you, 'Joo Lik-a hot penis?' He's tapping at the damned vending machine and you STILL had no clue what he was trying to say. He's all, 'Joo can try my hot penis.' He puts his money in the machine, makes his selection, pulls out this bag of hot peanuts and you scream, 'HOT PEANUTS!' He nods his head and says, 'Jes....Penis. Joo wanna try my hot penis?'"

"You know, I actually use that line sometimes on guys. If I'm not sure what side of the fence they're playing on I'll ask.... 'You like penis?' They'll go, 'Say what?' And that's my cue. "Peanuts. Do you like peanuts?"

As they laughed Meredith's eyes grew heavier. You could hear her breath labor to take wind. "Let's just suffice it to say that if all the people we ever came across were to meet, the room would explode....And thank you."

"For what?"

"For being my soul mate."

You could sense it beginning....or ending, rather.

Eric lowered his cowering eyes.

"I've been trying to push away the sadness I've been feeling lately, because I don't want to bother you with depression in your last days. Good Lord, that's the last thing I wanted to do was to make you feel sad. My eyes for the last two weeks have hurt. There is this pressure behind them, all these tears I keep pushing back. I know at some point I'm gonna have to admit to what's happening, but I'd rather not. I want things to be the way they were a few months ago. Just us laughing all the time, not even having to say anything. Just laughing." Eric smiled and slipped a chuckle in between the weltering tears. "All I had to do was just look at you and start laughing. Good God, you've got one of the most unbearably funny faces. But, I can't bare to look at you right now because I wouldn't laugh. I'd start bawling. I just keep thinking about what happens next....What happens when you're gone and I'm out by myself now. I'm gonna be so alone." He realized Meredith had not said anything and still he could not look to her direction. He didn't dare lift his stare from the linoleum floor, his eyes concentrated on the cluster of blue and gray flakes in the fake tile. "Meredith?"

No answer came.

Still, without looking at her, he tugged at her leg and said, "Hey....." his voice cracking somewhat. He made the beautifully noble attempt to smile, but the tears had begun to slowly show themselves. Still he did not look at her.

"Dammit," he whispered under his breath and stood, pulling

the nearly empty bottle of wine from her hands with his eyes looking about elsewhere. The remains of the Yellow Dog were sent down the drain of the bathroom sink. The empty bottles were put into the backpack and Eric moved around the room trying to discard any remnant that may have suggested he had once been in the room. And strange to see the metaphors play through psychology when someone close dies. The poor man never once looked at Meredith.

Before leaving, he remembered the bottle of Beaujolais that they had not gotten to. It was retrieved with trembling hands off the night stand before he quietly slipped out the door to inform the nurses that Meredith had died. Ball cap pulled down over the wet, painful eyes, and backpack clanging full of wine bottles, this sad little man with head bowed walked out of the hospital and into the world alone.

We like to think processions and funerals and all traditions that mark the passing of life are intended for the dead, but we are reminded when the truth of life, of it's loneliness sets in, that these productions of ceremony and show are exclusively for the living. Death reminds the living, not the dead, of the separatism and loneliness that now face those left behind. And Meredith's funeral was no exception. Although beautiful, it was eerily traditional, strangely normal. ANd perhaps because this distinct service for friends and family was the facade, whilst the real ceremony played on elsewhere.

Friends from across the globe came to say goodbye and even I made the drive out to pay my respects. The weather couldn't have been more agreeable and the church in which the service was held was distinctly Meredith. Slightly Gothic, non conventional and beaming with filigree and imagery. The hymnals sung by the choir were not sad, but reflective. When people dried their eyes, they did so more out of happy memories, rather than somber reflection. For with every tear you heard a chuckle, a laughter, a sigh for the good times. It was not long into the ceremony that I realized Eric was not there. Too some degree I was stunned, and disappointed. My first reaction and instinct told me that it was in very bad form for him not to have been there considering how close they had been. But, the more I thought about it, the more it was made clear to me that he simply could not handle a ceremony that did nothing but clarify for himself and all the world to see that Meredith, the friendship, and an enormous part of Eric's soul was now dead. I don't think he could have handled seeing a congregation of people remind him that he had forever lost that which had made him whole.

I discovered some time later through a mutual friend, that as the funeral service was being held, Eric was at home in his pajamas, sitting on the floor, blinds drawn, lights out, drinking the bottle of Beaujolais he had brought back from the hospital the day Meredith died......crying his eyes out finally for the first time. In some brilliant mindful try, I realized that was the true funeral ceremony for the one left behind. The symbolism uniquely perfect. No casket, no grand church. This ceremony spoke of truth. Darkness, loneliness....and a simple bottle of a favorite red wine.

No one saw Eric again. Oh, he's alive somewhere surely. I've seen clues. A distant relative of mine passed away not too long ago and was buried in the same cemetery Meredith was. To say my respects and just curiously feeling the need to see how well maintained her grave had been kept over the years, I wandered over to her resting place. I saw fresh flowers, the tombstone freshly dusted, and a small card dangling that said, "Happy B-Day. Rest in Peace until I get there. Batboy." In front of the flowers, just aside the tombstone was a replicated tombstone made of the same ceremonial granite, but much smaller in size. With pristine and clean engraving it said, "IN LOVING MEMORY OF CHEAP RED AND NEARLY DEAD."

Cheers.

GREGORY PATRICK

CARNAL CHARNEL

GREGORY PATRICK

You would think it absurd this fascination of hers with shadows that linger in the corner of the room; shadows that linger when no object is there to cast the interruption of light. I refer to ghosts, dear reader. Melanie adored them.

Now, Melanie may have been a very unnatural woman, but she was a much more impressive woman than any other I had ever met, for no other woman up to that point or since had that glance that was so possessed. Wide eyed and with this love for fear, I found Melanie Seidler erotically entrancing, and the only way to entice her was to frighten her with a true tale of terror. What turned her on, what made her hot, was not the chill and the iciness of any old thrill, but the things that leap and the things that creep from out of a storybook's darkness.

She said to me once, "The adrenaline when moving through you in one wave can be so sensual at times...." I can still recall that purr in the voice that is so singularly hers. "To have yourself stare at a scare can be the most addictive of confrontations for you feel your body tingle and your heart quicken to a pace that is deadly." Melanie is so very pleased by the revenants.

There is a house on our street with the most provocative rumor of haunt. Of course, our most stable of individuals would find the idea of specters creeping about a house quite silly. As was expected though, our Melanie took a particular liking to the story and begged me to tell her the tale over coffee one sensual spring eve...just we two.

Dressed in a reckless, neckless, crushed velvet gown of forest green hue she moved deeper into the candlelight's flickering flame. As that white spark licked her white skin I could not resist the desire to make her mine.

Melanie lit herself a cigarette, sipped her coffee anxiously with those eyes wide with surprise. The only sounds in the darkened room were my sly words, the whisper of winds through cracks in the window frames, and Melanie's heavy, hot and excited breath as she listened closely to the story of Benjamin and Sara, just recently married, who moved into the before mentioned house near Madison Square just three days after the final bricks and mortar and what not had been put into place. The house was a gift from Benjamin's father, an architect, who had for the longest time wanted to construct something family oriented, rather than some monolithic office structure (his everyday maneuver).

All was serene for the couple kept cozy in their lean two story home until one month after their picturesque wedding of soft colors and radiant smiles when the tragedies of eternal commitment began to occur. They had not even time to explore their love for one another yet when the simplest arguments would send them into terrific rows, when even the slightest of disagreements would send them soaring into attack.

"Leave the blinds open, would you please?" She was exploring a book, never taking her eyes from the page to make her request.

"Its so horribly sunny out there and I'd just like to take a nap."

"We need the fresh air in here, you're smoking has made the room smelly"

"You'll get your fresh air, I only want to take a nap and its too bright out for a good nap." Benjamin only paces, knowing full well the throttle of this conversation will quicken into an onslaught shortly. After all, he's attempting to antagonize her on purpose.

"Darling, you're probably too tired to notice if the blinds are open or not any ways, so what difference does it make? The smoke in here is like some low cloud that we just can't seem to get rid of and you do nothing but worsen the situation every time you light up one of those cancer sticks."

"Tell me, please, why every single detail has to be to your liking? Why does everything have to be your way? You know, you've changed Sara. I should be able to come home and take a nice nap without having to battle my wife. You've changed, Sara. You used to be so calm and relaxed, now you've gotten all goddamn stiff and meticulous."

"Me? I'm not the one whose changed." Slammed shut went her book. Now, now all her attention centered on attack. "YOU have! You've gotten all ragamuffin, you don't do anything to keep yourself tidy, reeking of stink and sweat and then falling into our bed sheets smelling like you'd been drinking! I need the fresh air! Your nastiness is suffocating me!"

'THEN GET OUT! If you need the fresh air so much, then just go out and waft for all I care! I want to take a nice long, smelly nap in the dark! Do you hear me? This conversation is over!"

"You're not being very cooperative, Benjamin!" His name said as profanity.

"How very perceptive, Sara!" Her name said as a reviled curse.

"Leave the blinds open!"

"Closed!"

"Open!"

"Closed!"

"Open, I say!"

"Damn you, they will stay closed!"

And so forth and so on until the two of them were simply too tired to carry on, spinning and stomping off in opposite directions. Rest assured, though, they would be at it again, bitching and bickering about what ever could possibly fit the moment.

It was likely that their marriage would end soon, with Sara sleeping upstairs in the bedroom and Benjamin sleeping down on the couch some nights and who knows where on other nights.

Benjamin would often wake very early to avoid a confrontation with his wife, leaving long before she woke and only returning once he was certain she was sound asleep. You see, there is something quite blistering about staring face to face with the one you despise, when once you had so adored them.

One Saturday morning the quarreling couple happened to run into each other as she was leaving to do some shopping and he was returning from a long night of far too much to drink, rumble-tumbles with the unsavory sort, and the occasional flirting with a less than sincere lady.

She asked him, to be quite honest, quite sincerely, "Where were you last night?"

"Out"

"Out where?"

"Out where wives don't go. None of your business."

Then something happened that Benjamin had never seen before and he knew for certain that it would cause a cataclysmic ripple within, for Sara had started to cry.

With wet cheeks and quivering lips she said, "Thank you for being so cruel when I was only worried about you."

129

She quietly closed the door behind her and slipped into the world.

Benjamin sat there on the floor just before the door staring at his wife's exit as it saddened him so. He put his face in his hands, hands that smelled of foul and rancid beer and far too much nicotine, and tried to desperately think of what had happened between the two of them. Could this have been prevented? Forget prevention, it is now time to seek some sort of cure.

He looks at her memory, her vision, with his eyes closed and sees something powerful and intense, but are these the same feelings from months before your wedding? The vision of her seems to fade, though, as hate and resentment have stood between the two lovers casting a shadow over their passion.

Looking upon Sara so long ago, Benjamin knew deep in his twisting belly that the two of them would love forever....or so had hoped. Spring is always dangerous for romance, and it was a sleeping Spring day when they first met at Forsyth Park. At their first meeting, Sara had worn one of those pastel dresses, a blue derivative or pink perhaps. Regardless, it was one of those nasty colored billowing things that Benjamin had always hated to see a woman in. But, with her stance and her gaze it was so beautiful. She had a smile that was a deeper darker shade than red, and a freckle spotted her nose here and there, whilst the sun cast a red halo to her brown hair. Meeting after meting it seemed only obvious that

Benjamin loved her and that Sara so adored him. The proposal was made four months after their first encounter.

"Live life with me together and forever always....."

"*Always.*" The word echoed in Benjamin's mind. He pulled his face from his hands, red eyes glaring, wet with sorrow and regret, and dashed for the door, swinging it open and calling her name. "Sara!"

But, she was gone, though, long since gone to do her escape for the day. When she would return, if she would return, she would find that Benjamin had gone through such great lengths to recapture the love that they had abandoned.

Their closest friends had noticed that their relationship was suffering. Their friends, and I use that word with much hesitation, had noticed that the relationship was spiraling towards an ending. Their neighbors had been recently pressing their ears against their walls and leaving their windows open just slightly enough to hear the arguments arise in the newlyweds little house...and God did the gossip ensue.

"I hear that Benjamin has turned to alcohol and he will devour just about anything with an octane that he can find, then slushes about like some mad man screaming about how windows ought to be left closed! And that poor, poor Sara! Benjamin is so drunk most of the time he can't even make it upstairs to bed. Its heart breaking to see a young girl having to sleep alone in such a big bed and they haven't even been married two months yet! They ought to be making children! They should still be honeymooning!"

"Mooning, did you say? He's been mooning people???"

"No, Dear. *HONEY*-Mooning! Really! You ought to pay attention! That's just how gossip gets started! May I have more tea please?"

"Well, you know I'm really not the sort to gossip, but I do prefer to share factual information, and your facts are all shamefully wrong. Benjamin isn't the one to blame. It's that woman he's married to. She married him for his money, you know. Have more tea, please. Benjamin does drink, but not nearly as much as you say. But, even if he did, it would only be to numb the truth that he is so desperately trying to deny. Sara goes shopping four days a week. You see? Do you see what I mean, dear???" A wink to urge on her counterparts imagination.

"Oh, my goodness! I stand corrected! She did marry him for the money then! Lemon, please."

"Dear, if we're not careful, we'll spread the worst sort of gossip possible! Listen carefully! She goes shopping....but doesn't return with any merchandise.....Do you see? You'll have to settle for cream, I haven't any more lemon." Another wink.

"An affair, you mean???"

"The sort that would make your head spin!"

"Sleeping with another man! Well I'm glad I got that cleared up. I would hate to think I was spreading rumors! By all means, pass the cream."

"You old women are so perfectly darling, but you don't know the truth as I do."

My interception into the conversation had offended the old biddies. I was so happy to have shut their wrinkled lips, their tea cups still yet to touch their cracked and crackled sneers.

"Well, then, if you know everything, do tell us why has their marriage failed then?" Asked one of the old crones.

"They fell out of love."

"Now, that is the most unbelievable thing I have ever heard of! I'm shocked at how willfully you wish to spread such lies!"

"It happens all the time. People fall in love, then people fall out of love. When the heart stops pumping the passion, when the dreariness in their discussions seem obvious, when neither of them has anything impressive to see in the other one, then they've fallen out of love. Its as simple as that. And actually quite common."

"And where was it that you heard this repulsive rumor?"

"You old hens creep close to your open windows, listening, analyzing and dissecting everything they're saying whilst I listen for what they have *yet* to say to one another."

"What is that?"

"*I love you.*"

When Sara returned home later in the afternoon, carrying

very many bags of merchandise, thank you, she was met with the surprising sight of her husband all dressed up and fit for formal dancing. He looked simply adorable in her eyes with his hair still wet and curling at the top of his ears. Benjamin stood staring with big brown eyes and fingers all fidgety.

The lump in his throat brought some hesitation, nonetheless, he asked anyway. "What did you do today?"

"I went shopping. Bought some knickknacks for the house. Little things, you know. Just stuff to make it more a home....."

"A home. Not a house."

"Big difference. A house is a building. A home is where love lives." Another one of the impressive reasons he had once been so attracted to her...She moves deeply in her passions.

"I see."

Sara noticed the well made suit designed precisely for his frame. "You're all dressed up. I hope you're not going out. I was hoping to talk to you."

"I was planning on going out. But, I was hoping we could go out together. You're right. We do need to talk."

"That's very strange. It's the first time we've agreed on anything since we've been married."

"So...."

"So."

"Where do we start?"

134

They started with a kiss.

Now, he was to have to taken her out to dinner, then a lovely stroll down River Street. But, up the stairs they went instead. Once Benjamin laid Sara on the bed he kissed her on the neck, then on the cheek and once more on the lips. When his mouth moved to hers the world ceased to turn. They made love in a fashion superior to that of simple sex of the body. The mind was touched, the soul was touched, and the body was truly lessened to the role of instrument and nothing more. The arousal of their desires came not from their bodies warmth, but from the silky movements of their smitten hearts.

Now, what happens next is what I believe to have happened that night formed not only from my own instincts, but from the newspaper reports that appeared after what we on this street call simply, "the damned murder."

A scream woke Benjamin with a gasp and a grasp at the spot next to him where Sara should have been sleeping, but there was nothing there. His heart fell from his body. Benjamin could see not a thing in the darkness but heard his name in shrieking tone that made muscles tighten. Catapulting with speed he made his way to the bedroom door to find only that it was locked. Just one spark of a second before he could unbolt the latch, a fiery fist knocked him groggily to the floor. A daze surrounded him and he shook his head with blistering confusion. This intruder, this man, this thing that had seeped from the shadows laughed so spitefully that the devil would have taken refuge. Benjamin could not see him, but he could hear the intruder whispering foul things in the darkness as he kicked Benjamin repeatedly in the torso.

"I don't fucking think you know what pain is, you fuck head. You and your fucking skin."

And again, the intruder once, twice, three times more kicked Benjamin's rib cage.

The pain caused Benjamin to vomit and blood stained his teary eyes.

Benjamin could hear Sara now pounding on the outside of the door, kicking at it and clawing at it with this chilling shake of trepidation. "Benjamin! NO! BENJAMIN! FIGHT HIM! FIGHT HIM!!!!"

But, he couldn't! No! The pain and the confusion were much too unbearable. The things spoken by the intruder were simply insane.

"I'll pull your skin from your skull and shove it down your throat, you sonofabitch."

As Benjamin tried to fight the intruder did nothing but laugh and kick and slap Benjamin hard across the cheek. In and out of his mind he barely noticed that he was now in the process of being hog tied and being rolled onto his belly. The intruder showed the long jagged edge of the blade to the helpless one as he pulled his hair

136

tight, exposing his neck. The blade was pressed against Benjamin's throat. Benjamin screamed for help from anyone outside in the neighboring houses, but no one heard a word....I know I didn't.

Sara was till fighting with the door, pounding against it, tossing the strength of her fear against it, screaming this sound that I can only think describable as the ultimate pain: *witness to the death of your loved one.*

With one slow and precise slice the intruder cut open Benjamin's back exposing blood and spine. The scream dulled then....Shock had overcome the victim. The sound of slicing was soon heard.

Sara fled the home and made her way to one of the elderly biddies who lived next door, one of those terrible women who was so consumed with what happened in the neighborhood. The old woman went into hysterics when she was met with the gruesome sight of Sara shrieking on her door step, "HELP ME! FOR GOD'S SAKE, HELP ME!"

The police arrived in absolute no time, but by this point, nothing could have been done to save poor Benjamin's life. Rushing up to the bedroom, the repulsion of the wicked scene sent the police retching, spilling over in disgust, and nearly fainting. Benjamin had been skinned alive...But, what horrified them most about the scene, what truly harmed their psyche from that moment forth was noticing that the skin had been force fed back to Benjamin, his skin having been shoved down Benjamin's throat.

We are good people on this street, you understand. This isn't the sort of derangement you should find near these homes of ours. For the longest that anyone can remember, the best names and the most astute of faces has made its way through our alleys and lanes. We are not the sort to attract this sort of misfortune. You can imagine how frightening and upsetting this incident was for everyone.

Sara never went back to that house. She spent the rest of her days in a hospital ward. They say she slept with her eyes wide open, as though she were transfixed in a trance that kept her constantly close to the events of that evening. When she wasn't sleeping, she was screaming, "HELP ME!"

The investigators into the crime could get no help from the now mentally ill-equipped Sara. They did their best to ask questions, but the woman simply stared, mouth agape...not the slightest twitch to convince anyone she was coherent or even rational. She died soon after, her body simply shutting down on her. Had she lived, there would have been no life for her to pursue anyway. Everything had been taken from her. Everything, I say, right down to her mind.

A spell blanketed over our little tree lined world that never ever went away. The flowers don't bloom as they should, and if they do, no one notices them. You can't walk within a block of that house of Benjamin and Sara's without feeling it, you see. You can still feel the energy of that grotesque evening all over you. We all tried for the longest time to squelch the power of that murder over all of us, but once the incident itself was over, we were all left to deal with the 'who' and the 'why' of that frightful night. Just a few days after Sara's death when we were convinced our street could not take a darker turn, it did....when we discovered that Benjamin had not been simply murdered. He had been executed.

There were issues the investigators quickly took notice off at the house. There had been no forced entry into the home. Furthermore, the killer's fingerprints had only been found on that one bedroom doorknob and no where else throughout the entire extent of the home. He had not even left his prints on any of the walls. How else could anyone have come to the conclusion that he had been *allowed* inside.

Another interesting fact to note from the moment the investigators arrived. Why was Benjamin locked alone in the room with Sara left outside? Had it been sheer coincidence that she had woke, left the bedroom and went downstairs? And had that been the case, then wouldn't she have passed the intruder? Wouldn't she have seen him?

Within time it was blurted out extensively in the newspapers the details surrounding a surprising affair and the resulting execution. Throughout the rough course in their marriage, Sara had taken on a lover who lived in Thunderbolt, a lowly man named Franklin who had not the money nor promise that Benjamin had, but who had wooed Sara with his physique and his abilities in the bedroom. She confessed to Franklin she could not love him, so to speak, but that the extent of their relationship was simply physical.

These words tell all, "Had I never met him, if Benjamin wasn't in my life, I could probably have a relationship with you, Franklin. But, he's my husband. And despite the hard times our relationship is having, I still miss having his body against mine, I miss the touch of his *skin* against mine...."

This was enough to set the lover into a rage as Sara left him there that last time. That would be the last night of a somewhat normal life for all those concerned. Deep in the evening a knock at the door pulled Sara from bed. Benjamin was too far asleep to have heard anything and continued to sleep peacefully. When Sara opened the door she found Franklin standing there who quickly moved his way inside.

"I need you, Sara, you can't back out on me."

"You shouldn't be here! He'll hear you! Do you understand! He'll here you! You have to go!"

"Don't leave me for that asshole, Sara! You can't."

Within moments the situation had reached a fevered pitch, the two of them trying not to shout. Franklin then grabbed Sara's arms and gripped at her forcefully. Those marks noticed by

140

investigators as she withered away throughout her remaining hospital stay.

"You want his fucking, stinking skin against yours??? That's what you want????"

He then spun her around and pushed her so hard into the wall that she lost her breath for a moment. Whilst she attempt to revive herself quickly, Franklin had already made it up to the bedroom. Sara screamed.....the door was locked....and the incident ensued.

So it had been revealed. We on this street were in awestruck at the complexity and deceitfulness in which Benjamin and Sara had lived their lives beneath our noses. And to those two old biddies who caught on long before the rest of us that something peculiar was going on in that affair, I could only say, "I stand corrected."

Franklin was convicted of the crime and died in prison awaiting his appeal.

"Oh, please! DO HURRY!" I was interrupted by Melanie who slapped at the arm of chair with her hand. "Get to the part about the ghosts! That's what I want to hear! I don't give a care about gutter trash and their scandals! Get to the ghosts!!!"

Yes, the ghosts. I never hold true to any story that insists, *"There are those who say,"* for it seems some can *say*, but none can confess to having *seen* anything. Not so in the case of Benjamin and Sara. We've all on this street seen it at least once. I myself have seen it twice.

There is never a forewarning to when it may happen. No weather pattern, no particular day. You're caught off guard completely. On some evenings "the incident" repeats itself all over again. You hear the sound of a door slam and a lock being bolted, the sound so amplified its like a calling to all who can hear that the grand ghostly show is about to begin. You can then see one shadow in that upstairs bedroom, being tossed about and beaten by an unseen thing. You hear the sound of the pummeling in reverse. You hear the screaming in dull droning slowness, you see blood splash against the window and the walls. And within no time you see the shadow stripped of its silhouette while trying to fight....what is left is emptiness and nothing, the sound of slicing heard again and again in reverse, this heavy grinding moaning, slow, and emanating the air. Just moments after that, you see the front door open and the ghastly hue of a white figure run out shrieking, "HELP ME!" before it reaches the edge of the lawn, dissipating into nothing. All grows quiet and as it once was, the entire episode lasting no more than two minutes or so.

I looked to Melanie, whose eyes were both sexually profound and round with the promise of interest. I was thoroughly aroused.

"You've seen it happen?" She asks teetering on orgasmic shrill.

"Twice, yes."

"TWICE! And is it gorgeous?"

"Ha! I doubt gorgeous is the word I would use. It is chilling, if not only for the fearful depiction of what happened that night, but for the fact that we on this street will never be done with that memory. Perhaps it's we who bring the demons back to repeat the torture and scream. Perhaps our own collective subconscious on this street can't let it go."

"Don't ever let it go!!! NEVER! It's wonderful!"

"There never was and never will be another quite like you, Melanie."

"Ah," she sighs, falling back into the comfort of the chair, sighing again with a smile and a bright leap back to attention. "I've heard that story a thousand times and no one can tell it quite like you can. Thank you, so much. I had to hear it at least once more...."

Now, there was a look in her eye that proved she was hiding something from me.

"Once more?"

She took a deep breath, put her hand at her chest and smiled at me with a brilliance that bordered on madness.

"Before I move in!" She said.

GREGORY PATRICK

TENENTS

FOR TOAST

I'm sure you're aware of the sort that puckers when they smoke? The Madam was no exception. She'd lazily gobble the filter down to the bitter end of her tongue to inhale and when she pulled the thing away driblets of saliva slipped from the toke. The Madam resembled a frog, or a toad, depending on what school of reptile you admire. A flat face stretched her eyes too close to her ears hidden behind years of split-ended hair flung back in a half hazard bun held in place by a pencil, chewed only when she had run out of cigarettes. She was indeed elderly, but should you ask for a precise age or even her birthday she would reply, "Why? What do you want? TO GIVE ME SOMETHING? I've been handed my fair share already. Don't concern yourself with me.....Incidentally, I know *your* birthday. And what you got. I know much much more than that, too. As a matter of fact, I know alot. Much more than you want me to...."

Tenants living beside the dear Madam rarely lasted. They were "forced" they often told the landlord, to vacate. An uncomfortable sense of gloom shadowed the little half of the duplex they let, thanks to the Madam and her lurking close by. They admitted repeatedly that they felt spied on. Not only that, but the most privy of chats was left wide open for anyone to know about, for the Madam made claim she knew their private dealings. She confessed to spouses of affairs, to children of impending divorces, to authorities of alleged abuse. She slunk along walls, the Madam did, and some of the better tenants could hear her.

Being the recluse that she was, the Madam had taken a fancy to keeping cats, as most hermits do, for the cat requires fairly less attention and needful walks outside your domain than a dog does. However, the cats she acquired through whatever resource or another (mostly hungry ones dropping on her doorstep) quickly left her once they discovered that she was inclined to bath them in the traditional feline matter. By this I mean she licked the cat as the cat would have licked itself. As frightening an idea as this may be, imagine the cats sense of violation when she would begin to slobber them with her wet ended tongue. Nonetheless, after one bathing (which the Madam was apt to do nearly DAILY), the cats would refuge themselves in whatever hidden corner or crevice they could find, never eating, never sleeping, but crouched in pensive pose waiting for the next moment the front door would open. Then and there would the cat in current question make a brake for it, forever outrunning the Madam and never returning. The occurrence happened so often, the gaining and losing of a cat, that the Madam all together stopped offering them names, yet instead insisted on calling them by their consecutive order in which she received and lost them.

"Tst! TST! Seventeen! Tst! TST! Oh, do come back you measly thing!"

By the time Thirty-Two was gone so were the latest tenants to have shared a wall with the madam. The young couple who had lived there just shy of three weeks were attempting to conceive children. The found they had an audience and were berated by a hidden voice from the other side of the wall door criticizing them of their copulatory moments....while the moment was occurring.

"Oh, for God's sake! Put your pelvis into it! She's not even moaning! Good God, man! Hump her!"

But, now the couple and Thirty-Two had decamped leaving the madam the only tenant in the building. Which gave the voyeuristic hermit the most ample opportunity to enhance her need to see just beyond her bordered wall before the next tenant arrived. To hear the goings on of a neighbor were one thing, but to see such a thing with crystal clearness was her intention. The landlord who owned the building usually had the secondary apartment rented within three days, which gave the madam a time or two to consider just the right spot for a pinhole along her living room wall for peeping. With a very long nail and a simple hammer she softly made a hole quietly into the drywall that separated her apartment from the next, spending hour upon hour with tongue lashing out often with glee when she would begin to see more and more of the room that was set beside her own.

And true to form the next apartment had been rented just one day after the Madam had prepared for herself a cushion beneath the pinhole to ease her squatting.

How delighted the Madam was to find a couple inside the little apartment inquiring with the landlord about its quiet state, its neighbors, its heat in the winter, its cooling ability in the summer. Her liquid tongue went thrashing out of a sly smile. She would have to wait no time at all to begin her proud bouts of spying.

Yes, the landlord assured the couple (him slightly more stout than his female companion, and she somewhat taller than he) that the breeze that swept through in late spring kept the apartment well cooled all through summer, and that the boiler room that kept the extent of the duplex tight and cozy in winter was just in the basement below this (a quick tap or two with his foot) floorboard.

The stouter young man of the couple said, "I think this will be perfect for my father."

He was "getting on in years," the woman now said.

To this the Madam cringed a little. "Father? What father? Oh, no no no, I don't want an old man!" She whispered to herself.

As the conversation between the couple and the landlord progressed it was sharply discovered that the couple had no intention of letting the apartment for themselves, but wished it on the behalf of their ailing father.

"Damn! Now he's AILING, too???" Shouted the Madam noticeably, and all three on the other side of the Madam's pinhole looked in various direction for where the shout had come from, but all three quickly shrugged the moment as though it had never happened at all.

The Madam had no desire to spend all this time and energy dropping to stoop before the pinhole for the sake of a dying old man. How boring! Not to mention the pain elevating herself back up off the floor was far too much to handle for no reason at all! Oh, her head dreaded at the thought of seeing the tell tale signs of age through the pinhole. "I won't crouch all the way down here to watch scraggly nurses change his cholostemy bags!" The more she thought of it, the more angered she became. "Well, I'll just have to find some way to get THIS one to scurry on, too!"

The day soon came when she heard the rumblings of furniture being moved in the apartment next door. The Madam was in the kitchen poaching an egg and dared not leave her station to listen, nor dare spend the time crouching down to her pinhole. "I hope his walker slips right out from underneath him!" All said while pouring vinegar into the boiling water and sipping on the most ill fermented cheap wine those on a budget can find.

She huffed at the *THUDS!* from the next room, twitched when she heard *THUNKS!* and did her best sigh and rolling eyes routine when ever she heard something *SCREECH!* against the hardwood floors. "I'll have to do my best to get you out of there soon, old man. If not for your sake, then for the landlord's floors!"

That was when her resilience faded and she plopped herself down with the aching strains old ladies make when dropping to the floor. "I'll have to dig up something on you, old man." With poached egg on toast in hand, and bottle of wine at her side, she spied through the pinhole to find whatever nasty business there was about this old man that could satisfy a quick and immediate eviction.

The Madam was taken by surprise.

"He's not *that* old. Hmmm....Not bad looking, really." Though his hair had long since left him, his skin was tanned with the leathering remains of summers past and his physique wasn't tripped and frail, but still quite tight if but a little worn with age. But, the conversation the Madam had over heard had been about him "ailing," and to this the Madame was perplexed. "Must be something I can't see."

The movers were leaving just about the time the Madam finished her egg, the couple leaving not long after them, too, leaving the man (we can't really call him "old" anymore) alone in the apartment, standing perfectly still for a brief moment or two.

The man moved with a soft and slow approach to the great window that over looked his street. With a timid grace that resembled the gentleness of meditation and of steadiness, he raised

152

both arms to either side of him, the long fingers of a piano playing man stretching out very slowly to caress the drapes, then quickly as if conducting an orchestra to silence itself, drew the curtains closed, leaving the living room quite dark, and the Madam straining herself on one knee to see better through the pinhole.

The man then cautiously moved to his simple brown couch, taking careful attention to where he stepped. He inspected the couch, pacing at its seating, peering down as if inspecting the cushions as though they were soldiers. Then he paused, bent over slowly, and began to pick with just the precise edge of his fingertips little bits of nothing more than lint and dust, or perhaps a crumb or two.

"So that's what they meant by 'ailing.' He's losing his mind." The Madam watched him with fascination.

Again the man paces the extent of the couch, now circling it, now finding his way to the center of it, brushing the center cushion once more. Slowly he turns on his heels, his cautious stead a simple eloquent swivel, then he abruptly plops down onto the cushion with the applause of dust billowing from out of very seam.

He sat there for a very long time. This gave the Madam plenty an opportunity to scan the extent of the room with that one eye gleaming through the pinhole. Everything was brown. The couch, the curtains, the rug, the bookcase....and yes....the more she squinted she could see, each of the books on the book case had been recased in brown bags from the grocer. A simple 40 watt bulb swung tenderly from side to side from the center of the room casting brown shadows on the man's brown clothes. The man would slowly turn his head from side to side, the eyes always a step ahead from the chin's position. The Madam stared at him in awe.

"He's definitely ailing, alright. Ailing right into the looney bin." She said this last bit just a little too loud.

The man's big brown eyes darted in her direction. The Madam sat petrified. Mr. Brown, as she was beginning to refer to him in her mind, stood to attention sharply, ran to the pinhole and shouted, "BOO!" The Madam lunged back onto her strained knee screaming.

"Who are you! WHAT ARE YOU DOING THERE!" Though the Madam could not see, the man was pacing back and forth before the pinhole.

"You're mad, I tell you! MAD!"

"And what you're doing is criminal!"

He had a grumbly, rough voice, a gravely voice that sounded.....brown.

"I'm doing no such thing! I....I...decline to have a conversation with someone whose mentally ill! Oh, dear God! I'm no criminal! I- I-*I can't get up!*"

"You must be fat!"

"How dare you insult me!"

154

"Or old...."

"Oh, that's enough out of you! Now, you may be crazy, but you can at least be a gentleman and see that I've lost the use of my knee! It's gone out! I CAN'T STAND!"

"And that's why you're on the floor?"

"YES! And I was about to ask for help through the pinhole before you charged for me!"

"Hmmmm."

"Now, do be a good neighbor and come 'round and help me to my feet."

"I can't."

"What do you mean, you can't? Don't be preposterous."

"Is there anyone I can call to come assist you?"

"No! There's no one. Oh, for goodness sakes, come over and help me."

"Nope."

"Why not?"

"Because I have no intention of leaving this apartment."

"DON'T BE LUDICROUS! You'd rather my sit here and suffer?"

"I offered to call someone for you."

"Oh, bother!"

"So, if its a bad knee then you must be old...."

"Say nothing more! GOOD NIGHT!"

The Madam rolled herself away from the pinhole to sleep with pierced angry lip all throughout the night, crouched as an embryo seething on the floor.

By morning her knee was moveable, but the cramped and tense position she had slept in all evening had now left her back squarely out of place. She had to crawl to the kitchen, reach high for the refrigerator door to catch herself some milk, but spilled it. And insisting as those on a very poor budget tend to do, decided not to waste one bit, and lapped it up off the very floor.

"I say," said the voice from the other side of the wall, "you look something like a cat. A mangy old stray cat."

"I beg your pardon?"

"This pinhole works both ways, you know. I can see you clear as day. And I was right, you are old. I wouldn't call you fat.....just a little plump."

"Is this how my day and MY LIFE are supposed to be from now on? You casting insults at me from that pinhole?"

"I watched you pout on the floor all night. You were pissed. I got the best of you."

"So now you're spying *on me?*"

"Isn't that what you were doing?"

"If I was, then it was only for the better good of this building so that I know what kind of riff-raff has moved in. I could hear all the damage you were doing to that gorgeous apartment's floors."

156

"Gorgeous? For someone whose been spying over here you certainly haven't been looking at the apartment. Its filth!"

"Now I insist. My back is now thrown."

"It's from being old."

"Now will you stop that! PLEASE! My back is thrown and I cannot get up! I beg of you to come here and help me to my feet."

"I can't."

"You won't! You're insufferable!"

"No, I said I can't....there is a difference."

"Oh, so you're locked in are you?" She said sarcastically.

"That I am."

"The door locks from within the apartment, you ninny! Not to mention, I don't recall the landlord changing doors in the last few days. So, you're not locked in."

"But, I am.....But not by bolts and such, old woman. I'm locked in by fear."

The Madam softly shut her eyes and remembered once again the "ailing" part of the young couple's conversation. This combined with his strange compulsive monotonous behavior gave a sense of eureka to it all. He couldn't come to her aid. His fear wouldn't let him. The Madam understood and paused before saying anything and when she did speak, despite all of her rude ill mannered upbringings, tried to sound polite and concerned. She wanted to know more, and this could be from having legitimate concern, or from simply being a voyeur. Being accommodating would pull the truth from him more than badgering would. "Are you afraid to leave your apartment?"

There was no sound from the other side.

"Sir, are you alright?"

"Of course I am."

"Then, are you... *afraid* to leave?" Her voice was gentle and tender, gravely cautious of showing even the most annoyed of emotions.

"Yes. But, with that face of yours, aren't you?"

"If I were able to stand to my feet, I'd walk straight out that door."

"And do what?"

"For one, I'd come right over there and give you a fat lip for being so rude to me." So much for gentle and soft spoken.

"I always feel it best to be honest. One thing I assure you of, is that I will not lie."

"Why are you afraid of leaving your apartment?"

"Because I don't like people. I have no interest in them. Never have. I want to be left alone and I don't want to be bothered."

"Then why bother me?"

"You seem simple enough. There's nothing special about you and you're about my age."

"Sir, it is best to refer to a lady as though she were younger than you."

"I told you I wouldn't lie to you."

And to this she could not rebuke. Yes, he did say he wouldn't lie, she thought. *Now what else will he tell me.*

She creeped over on her crooked knees to the pinhole.

"Despite your disrespect for ladies, I'll behave and show you how much more mannered I am than you. I'll say it properly since I'm now here...Good morning."

"Good morning."

"Why do you hate people?"

"I thought we were starting off rather nice. Why do you have to go and quiz me so quickly?"

"Very well. Fine. We're being cordial. My name is-"

"What difference does it make what your name is. It's not like I'll confuse it with the other people in my grand social circle."

She was quickly getting irritated, but with a breath or two was able to tame it, suppress it, save it for some other day.

"I call you Mr. Brown."

"Why?"

"Because everything in your apartment is brown."

"Happen chance."

"Oh, I don't think so. There's something to that, everything being brown."

"I like the color. Is that harmful?"

"No....just odd."

159

"Why?"

"Well, because of all the colors in the world one would stick by through thick and thin and make their only acquaintance, brown would have to be the most.....oh, that's it! It's the most *boring*. It isn't cheerful it isn't warm, it isn't dark and depressing, its simply boring! Brown doesn't make you think of anything other than brown."

"Something like that, yes."

"I'm awfully good at figuring people out, you know."

"Good for me. I won't have to say anything, just here on my side of the wall and agree with you."

"Tell me about your children."

"They're adults, not children. They have lives of their own."

"Well, you couldn't have always been afraid to leave your apartment, something must have triggered it."

"Do you mind?"

"Well, you obviously met your wife outside, didn't you? and had a job, I imagine."

"Enough old woman."

"Call me Madam."

"Madam, spare me your hilarious analysis of me. I'm sure I've heard it before from my doctors."

"Why were you peeking at me thought the key hole this morning."

"I watched you quite a bit of the night. To see if you were all right."

The Madam's hand subconsciously rose to her chest and she smiled. Indeed, she was grateful. "Well, thank you. I'm touched."

"I didn't say I'd go that far."

"Are you sure that you're afraid of people? Or is it the other way around?"

"Are you sure there isn't someone I could call for you to get you off that filthy floor and away from this pinhole."

She didn't answer.

"You don't have any family?"

"No," she said with a stammer.

"Ah! How the tables turn! HA! I'm starting to understand *you*, Madam."

"What do you mean?"

"That's why you have a pinhole like this. You have to quietly invite yourself into people's lives, like it was television. Why not buy a television?"

"Because none of its real."

"But watching other people, in their most intimate settings, makes you feel like you belong with them, that you're involved in their lives, doesn't it? My my my, I guess I've learned alot from all my visits to the head doctor. Look at me, analyzing a mental case."

"I beg your pardon, I'm no such thing!"

"Oh, come of it, old woman! You have an affliction like I do. You're afraid of being alone. So to forget about being alone you escape into other people's lives, so you don't have to think about you're own."

"At least you have your children....and I imagine you're a widower, even though you refuse to talk about it."

"You're a peeping tom!"

"No, Mr. Brown, I am a voyeur."

"Candy coat it with French, you're still a peeping tom."

"So, what if I am. At least I'm not losing my mind."

"We'll see."

"Well, if you're not going to help me to my feet then I ought to at least try myself."

"That's the spirit!"

"Piss off old, man."

And with much determination, and much squealing and cursing to boot, the Madam did eventually raise herself off the ground with the arm of a nearby chair. A tremendous smile leapt into action and she turned round to the pinhole to gloat. "I don't need anybody, let alone *want* anybody," she said to herself.

With the glory that the sun can perfect in a human, morning made hasty brilliance throughout the Madam's apartment, filling whatever square it cut with the floating of dust and ash.

"I'm going to go to the market, Mr. Brown. Shall I get you

STORIES INSPIRED BY SIOUXSIE

anything?"

"My, what good manners you have, Madam. No, thank you."

"Very well, I'll return later."

"I'll be here," said his voice drifting as he moved further from the pinhole, from the wall.

And to this remark the Madam felt something akin to warmth. Had she made a friend? They certainly did not begin their acquaintance with pleasantries, but in fact, aren't people who are completely comfortable with each other often dismiss pleasantries to make way for honesty? Pleasantries are simply social graces for perfect strangers. And these two were simply *perfectly strange.*

The Madam went on with her day, with whatever errands needed her attention and did so with no hurry, no fuss, no quick need to be back at her pinhole. Mr. Brown would indeed be there.

Later, as she began making herself dinner (she would call it such, you and I would call it a can of corned hash, heated and salted to bearable levels), she called to the wall, for Mr. Brown.

"Mr. Brown? I say, Mr. Brown?" She tapped once or twice on the wall. "Mr. Brown, are you there? Well, of course, you are. Hello?"

"You're interrupting my reading, Madam."

"I just wanted to ask how you found dinner. Is it brought to you? Do you cook? How are you tending to yourself when it comes to food?"

"I eat, Madam.....and read."

"I was just concerned. I figured you must eat. Everyone must eat. I just didn't know how you survived and such when it came to your dinner."

"My cupboard is stocked for a month. And on the fifth of next month my son will bring me another stock. I'm fine, Madam."

"As long as you're fine."

"I am."

She went back to her kitchen to open her can, but went back to the wall with a hobbling sprint. "Mr. Brown?"

"Can't you see I'm reading?"

"Actually, no. I don't dare get back down there just now to the pinhole. My back, you see. I'm not plopping down there until I'm good and ready."

"What is it, Madam?"

"I have a present for you."

"For me? What on earth for?"

"A house warming gift."

His voice was now no longer distant but on the very other side of the wall.

"Madam, that's very kind of you. Unnecessary, but kind. What is it?"

"I tell you what. Meet me at the pinhole later this evening, after I've had my dinner and bath and I'll tell you. That way, I won't have to worry about getting back up again if I don't have to."

"Very well."

The Madam ecstatically (and with a hum!) went back to preparing her dinner. She rested on the bar stool that served as her usual perch for eating from the kitchen counter and flipped on her radio, now humming along with whatever song passed through the speakers. The madam then had a cigarette while listening to Schumann. She carefully bathed herself afterwards, primping and preening herself to acceptable levels. Perhaps to impress Mr. Brown? She found her best brooch (not the best by common standards, but her best, nonetheless), and her best stockings (reserved for weddings she was never asked to attend), and a nice ivory comb used to keep back her wiry hair. She dusted off a shawl she had crocheted for herself with yarn she had recovered from a trash bin and draped it over her shoulders, smiling at herself in the mirror with such pride. The Madam felt she looked beautiful, and perhaps she was. Physically, one has their own depiction about what beauty ought to be. Any philosopher or poet could attest to that. But, here, this strange old Madam's peculiar exuberance and happiness made her rightly beautiful.

Before leaving her bedroom she stopped at her dresser to fumble through some photographs she kept in the top drawer. To this one peculiar photograph she smiled with reminiscence then snatched another quickly from the drawer. The Madam carefully placed them in her bosom, grabbed her a bottle of whiskey from the kitchen, and went to meet Mr. Brown at the pinhole.

She had figured all day the best way of getting down to the pinhole and had carefully rehearsed it numerous times with mathematical precision. She turned her back to the wall until her whole body was firmly flush. With one hand holding the bottle of whiskey, and the other hand holding an ashtray, she lowered herself with a squint down to the cushion. Then she placed the whiskey and ashtray down, rolled her legs under her and comfortably leaned against the wall.

"Mr. Brown, are you there?"

"I am, Madam."

"What do you think?"

"Of what?"

"Of the way I look, Mr. Brown."

"I can't see very much of you. You're too close. I can only see your eye. Awfully red, if you ask me."

"Oh, bother!"

"You'll have to step back if you want me to see you."

She rolled her eyes and sighed. "Very well."

The whole business of rehearsing her way down had not been met with a return to her feet. She had not thoroughly thought about that. So, the grand act down to the ground was done in reverse....minus the whiskey and ashtray. Oh, how painful it was. Here lately, the Madam had taken more notice of her knees and back failing her and no movement was more reminding of that then trying to get up off the floor. But, she did so, despite what pain shot through her legs, nor through her spine, she rose up off the floor dutifully. "He'd better say something nice," she thought. "Or I'll knock his door down and beat him senseless."

She took two steps back from the wall. "Well?"

"You'll have to go a step or two farther. I can only see your bosom."

She did so, nearly knocking into the end table.

"Ah! I can see you now! Madam, you look very nice this evening."

"Oh, thank you!" She said exuberantly. "I didn't want to have to kill you."

"What?"

"Nothing. I'm coming back to the pinhole."

Once she was resettled, Mr. Brown asked about the gift.

"I left it outside your apartment door this afternoon."

"You do realize that I cannot go out there, don't you?"

"Not even to fetch my gift?"

"No."

"You don't have to leave, you simply have to open the front door."

"No."

With compassionate grace reserved only for the most worthwhile of Buddhist devotees she asked, "Good Lord, Mr. Brown. Is your condition that bad?"

"It is."

"What happens when your son brings your food?"

"I go into the bedroom until he's closed the front door completely behind him."

"I had no idea. I'm so sorry, Mr. Brown. I wanted to lift your spirits, give you a gift and make you feel welcome. Perhaps I could slide it under the door?"

"I beg your pardon?"

"I believe I can slide your gift under the door."

"What did you get me, woman? A pancake?"

"You'll see! I think I can!"

She screeched, but bolted up from her cushioned crouch beside the pinhole and rushed as quick as the invalid could to the front door, swinging it open, then taking the simple two steps to Mr. Brown's apartment door and managed to squish, bend, flatten, and pass the housewarming gift between the threshold and the door. She knocked once. "Its through!"

The Madam then retreated back to her own abode, sliding once more down the wall with ease to see through the pinhole Mr. Brown admiring a very brand new, unused, clean as could be, brown paper bag.

"Madam," he said smiling back at the pinhole, "Madam, it's perfect. Thank you!"

"It's for your books."

"Yes, it is. Its got very nice creases, don't you think? Thank you, Madam, thank you."

With the diligence his condition requires of him he brushed it off a number of times, blew off excess dust, and folded it carefully, oh so carefully into a small, neat square and tucked it between two other books on his case, those two books the exact same size, and both encased in brown paper bags. When Mr. Brown was through, he turned back and sat aside the pinhole.

"It was most kind of you, Madam."

"It was nothing, Mr. Brown."

And you see here sentiment meaning so much to those who require nothing from people and nothing from things. Sentiment relies only on its attachment to memory, to thought, to emotion. Sentiment needs no moment of celebrity, no exquisite expense. Sentiment needs only understanding a connection between the metaphysical and the real. A brown paper bag did Mr. Brown much more care to the soul than could have any priceless gem.

As he nestled down aside the pinhole he caught a whiff.

"I whiffed something."

"I beg your pardon, Mr. Brown?"

"I whiffed....(Sniff sniff). There's booze on your breath, isn't there?"

"Your nose is very good. HA!"

He could see her red eye lean back, could hear the gulping take a swig.

"Madam, what have you there?"

"Whiskey."

"Irish?"

"Goodness! HA! I can't afford Irish whiskey, Mr. Brown."

"Still...I bet it beats plain water."

"I'd offer a taste, a whole drink if you wanted, but...."

"I'll fetch a straw," he said with the first giggle she had heard from him.

"You laugh like a child, like a five year old blown into an old man."

"What? I can't hear you."

However, she could hear the rough rumbling of him ripping open drawers.

She said, "You always come across as so neat! It sounds like such a racket in there. Are you tearing the place apart?"

"For whiskey, I'd rip down the wall. My son won't buy it for me. I imagine he gets some control fetish out of it."

In a short moment he returned. The Madam sat on her side of the wall, watching a very long straw come provocatively through the pinhole. "Goodness," she said. "You mean business."

"Guide me, Madam. Place it in your bottle."

The Madam did so with wide eyes and smile. It was to be a party, indeed. "Sip! You're in! Sip!"

Mr. Brown did more than sip, he slurped! "Eh, now! I haven't all that much! It took a lot for me to save for this. Pace, Mr. Brown! Pace!"

"Oh, no, Madam. I wish to indulge (ah!) immediately!"

The two laughed as specters do once they've possessed the remains of the innocent. Dryly, short of cackling, they continued on for some while.

"I can't believe your son won't buy his own ailing father a simple bottle of whiskey. Whiskey might do you some good! Does me better than a doctor ever did."

"The boy's a prude! Do you need a Bible, by the way? He always seems to have plenty of those. They're all over him. Give another sip, won't you? They're all over him, in any pocket he's got. Little one's, big one's. He shits Bibles."

The Madam screeched a roar of laughter. "You're blasphemous, Mr. Brown! I love it!"

"He takes after his mother. Or 'took,' rather."

"You've mentioned your wife."

"Yes, and its no work of yours. That information is solely on behalf of the whiskey, Madam."

"Was she religious, too?"

"Insanely. I should have committed her first! But, alas...I didn't need to."

"Is she now gone, Mr. Brown?"

"Do we have to do this now? Here, give us more whiskey."

"If it will get you to open up."

"Don't you understand, Madam? I've grown quite comfortable getting to know you. Time stands still here at this ridiculous pinhole you made. Do you see? There is no past, no future....just some crazy old woman with whiskey. I don't want to think about the past and I don't dare step into the future. I want right now and only right now all the time."

"Is that part of your illness, Mr. Brown? That you fear change, things moving on? Is it all just an overall fear of death? Your paranoia, are they just a fear of death?"

Mr. Brown said nothing.

"Very well, I'll ask no more about it. Would that suit you?"

"Indeed it would....and so would more whiskey."

Again the bottle was lifted to meet the straw. With the bottle dwindling, any attempt at getting the straw to reach the liquor proved fruitless. But, in all this, the two laughed an awful lot at the absurdity of it.

"Mr. Brown?" The Madam was lowering her head beneath the tilted bottle, should any of the whiskey slip away and not be wasted. "Do you have an objection to this pinhole being any bigger."

"Bigger, did you say? Hmmm. How much bigger?"

"Not that much bigger, really. Just big enough to pass through a bottle of whiskey."

Mr. Brown laughed. "I knew it! You're slowly trying to worm your way in here, aren't you!"

"Only if you decide to keep that bottle on your side."

"Big enough for the bottle, you say." He paused briefly, then shouted, "Bah! Why not?"

"Have you a hammer on your side?"

"I do. Somewhere."

"Then you ought to do it. Carry on, Mr. Brown while I use the ladies room."

Mr. Brown moved into his kitchen where one seems to always have that one singular drawer containing no item in it suitable for a kitchen. Mr. Brown's junk drawer was as most filled with everything and anything totally unrelated to cooking, but what made his remarkably different and distinct was that every piece of junk in it was lined single file and in nice tidy order. He grabbed his hammer and a nearby pencil and went to the pinhole. Clearly, he thought, a bottle of whiskey held vertically must be about 10 inches, possibly 14 with room to spare. With one eye squinted, Mr. Brown circled a space about 15 inches in diameter around the pinhole, then brushed off the head of the hammer, blew on it for good measure, then swung.

A sudden crash knocked the Madam nearly clean off the toilet with shock.

"What on earth???? Mr. Brown?"

She tidied herself quickly then made way for the living room, back to the pinhole. She lowered herself in the back-flush fashion that had become second nature and looked through. "Oh, Mr. Brown! I assumed you were going to use a hammer, not a wrecking ball!"

Mr. Brown sat on his side of the wall, on his knees, the hammer dangling from his elder hands, his eyes twitching away the dust of drywall. "I can't believe it." He had managed with one single blow to knock a whole three feet wide onto his side. "This cheap wall couldn't have handled a fly swatter!" The one inch distance between his sheet rock and the Madam's wall showed age and despair, the pains of a decaying building.

"Mr. Brown, are you alright?"

"Its not like any of it crashing on me might have hurt me! It's practically paper! Its awful! Such a terrible building, no wonder the rent is so damned cheap!"

"I mean, you're affliction, Mr. Brown. Will a big gaping hole cause panic with your illness, Mr. Brown?"

"Why, I don't plan to go through it, Madam!"

"Just checking. Now, what shall I do?"

174

"Do you have another bottle of whiskey? I'd hate to think all this destruction was simply for one measly sip or two of that crummy whiskey."

"Of course there's another bottle. You get two for the price of one at the Indian market."

"That would explain the funny aftertaste. Go fetch that bottle while I crash through your wall, madam. I wouldn't want any of this crappy sheet rock hitting you in the eye."

She did as was instructed while Mr. Brown went just tapping at her wall as large chunks splintered off and hit the floor.

"Goodness," said the Madam.

"Ah, you see? I just barely swiped at it and it comes crashing down."

Within the span of just a few seconds a hole nearly the size as his own was made on the madam's side of the wall, two feet up from the floor and approximately three feet wide in size.

Mr. Brown laughed. "Hell, you could pass an entire still through here."

"What about your privacy, Mr. Brown?"

"What about yours?"

"I'm a voyeur, Mr. Brown. I don't believe in privacy."

"I'll think of something, I'm sure. Well, what are you waiting for? Pass me that bottle!"

The bottle was passed through.

"Cheers," said the Madam. "To the tearing down of boundaries!"

"Ah, yes, Madam. Cheers."

"Oh, I forgot all about these! Here, look!" She reached into her bosom to get the photographs. "These are photographs from when I was a performer!" Now, by 'performer' one might think theatre, dance, song.....Not so. The Madam was a burlesque performer in her time of prime. One photograph was of her lounging on a settee coyly hiding her womanly business with a feather boa while drenched in a bloodbath of red light. The other was of her stark naked, save the snake she petted between her thighs. "I was quite a looker!" Actually, this also is in the eye of the beholder. The Madam wasn't a great beauty, by all accounts, but it is doubtful that her past admirers had ever even noticed her face. Her assets are usually concealed by the most proper of persons while in public.

"Madam, these are highly inappropriate photographs.....I love them."

"Oh, thank you, Mr. Brown!"

"What a God send to have a neighbor like you, I'll say! You old woman! Seducing me with whiskey and dirty photos as if I were still a boy!"

"You could be a little easier, you know."

He looked over the photos once or twice with admiration before handing them back. Now, this sort of admiration had very little to do with her nudity, nor whatever arousal it may have done for a man his age, but this admiration came from some sort of shield blasted away in much the same way the wall between them had been easily torn down. She hadn't always been an old woman, she had a past, a life, a different one than most, a somewhat scandalous and exciting one and the fact that she was proud of it is what admired him. She held no regrets apparently about the woman she had been, and seemed to take an awful lot of pride in having been a 'performer.'

"How long did you perform?"

"For as long as I could."

"Until you were married, I suppose?"

"Oh, no, I never married." She now was showing her vulnerability and her own hesitance at sharing emotion. For she looked away from the wall and said, "Men didn't marry women like me. They weren't interested in what we said, or what we thought, or if we had an emotional side. Men used us for self gratification, then married women they could be seen with in a church. No, I never married. But, it's as it should be I guess. I'm far too stubborn and independent. I would never allow a man to control me."

"Yes, I agree. Without men chasing after you you could concentrate on performing."

"HA! Mr. Brown, you make it sound like it was a career."

"Surely you must have made some money."

"Yes. Millions, Mr. Brown, and I live like this to confuse people and scare them off."

"Bah!"

"I made enough money for a place to live, the costumes, and food and drink. But, there was never really enough to ever put in the bank. I guess I thought I'd never get old. And I did get old! I couldn't believe it! I looked in the mirror one day to find this shriveled gravity stricken creature staring back at me. Eyes sunken in and haggard, my tits well on their way to my knees, my hunching over more and more pronounced. I looked like I had shrunk, too! Like I was becoming a dwarf! I could no longer perform. I held out as long as I could, though. I was 55 when I retired."

"What did you do then?"

"I entered the exciting world of cash transaction and high finance. I was a grocery check out clerk until my knees, my back and my age kept from being able to stand for too long. The employer was kind enough to give me some sort of retirement, but it wasn't enough to live on. I'm sure you're aware, Mr. Brown, how expensive getting old can be."

"Yes, yes, indeed."

"So, I live mostly on social services. You're tax dollars paid for that whiskey."

"Damned good thing my tax money's going to where its needed!"

178

To this they both toasted.

"Oh, Mr. Brown, I do believe I'm exhausted."

"I second that."

"I think I shall have to sleep here on the floor."

"What on earth for?"

"Say I did make it up to my feet....I think I'm far to drunk to make it to bed. I'll be fine."

"Won't your back be hurting you in the morning."

"Ah, well...It doesn't really matter. I've had such a wonderful evening, I doubt I would care. Goodnight, Mr. Brown!"

"Goodnight, Madam."

She laid herself on the chilled wooden floor and and curled up to the cushion, which now became a make-shift pillow. With one heavy sigh, the Madam appeared to have succumbed to the drunken planes of euphoria and passed out.

Mr. Brown sat there for some time with his own thoughts, watching her through the hole in the wall. A sympathy developed for her quite gradually.

The poor woman had been spent by the world, then dished out of it like a nasty sponge soggy with filth. Perhaps it was an idea, a system in his head that reminded him that she, despite whatever damnation she had been put through, still had an enormously positive disposition. Mr. Brown could never claim that same remarkable fortitude, for he had all but shut himself away from the

179

world. He knew it, needed no therapist to remind him of it and even more, Mr. Brown was happy with it. Or was he?

Now, he recalled visions about his wife that led him to cringe and often to sigh. Now, she had not died, mind you, as one might imply by her absence. She had in fact left the old man at a time he was convinced all was right with life. And to that he never forgave himself, nor did he forgive concepts of happiness and joy, for they can be eerily tainted by someone else's selfishness. And thus, one can see by Mr. Brown's peculiarities that he wished things to remain as they are: always one mood, always one color, always one day that never becomes a second, nor a third. He had painstakingly contrived a bubble around himself that change could never enter. Alas, the Madam seemed willing to comply with the wild ideas Mr. Brown prized.

"She's sleeping on the floor," he whispered to himself. "She's willing to sleep on that rotten, filthy floor."

"I am, Mr. Brown."

"I beg your pardon?"

"I can hear you whispering."

"You shouldn't be eavesdropping."

"But, its what I do, Mr. Brown."

"Very well....Why are you willing to sleep on that floor anyway?"

"So that I may enjoy your company."

180

She lifted herself to an elbow and turned to the hole in the wall. "You're rather fun, Mr. Brown. I enjoy your company very much."

"Madam, you're not the tenant I expected living next door."

"Neither are you.... So, I guess we're both screwed."

Mr. Brown laughed with the Madam chiming in with bellows of her own.

"You ought to get some proper sleep, Mr. Brown. I'm likely to keep you up at all hours of the night. I'll have to get more whiskey tomorrow, so we can have another night like this."

"Ah, yes. I should sleep and prepare for more drinking tomorrow."

Mr. Brown said, "Goodnight, Madam!" And curled himself into a ball right there on his side of the wall.

"Mr. Brown, you can't be serious. Go to your bed!"

"I'd rather stay here. And I'm not to be bossed about. Now to sleep with you, old woman."

The Madam smiled, turned back to the floor, and smiled a flash of damaged nicotine stained teeth.

* * *

Mr. Brown could smell it.

Groggily his head lifted from the floor, the right side of his wrinkled head fraught with a numbness. His old eyes spied through a squint a bright light from the hole in the wall. From there he could smell it.

"What on earth are you doing to that food, Madam? It smells awful!"

"Its not so bad, really. It's perfect for a morning soaked with the pains of the previous evening's whiskey. My, I sound poetic, don't I?"

"Yes. You should stick to words and leave the kitchen alone."

"I've already had breakfast. This one's for you."

She stumbled to the hole in the wall.

"I barely made it up off the floor this morning, but I was damned if I was going to piss myself in my frock. So, up I got! And I got busy."

She passed a plate through the hole. Mr. Brown flinched. Poverty and experience have led the Madam to determine the most nourishing, if not beneficial breakfast after a night of drinking would be fried pork fat, a poached egg, and a piece of toast cut in odd shapes. "Why is it cut like that?"

"What, Mr. brown?"

"The bread. It's cut all strange. Is it supposed to be a star?"

The Madam peered through the hole and laughed. "Ha! I suppose it could be! No, it wasn't on purpose. That's where I cut the mold off."

"Oh, dear God. The mold?"

"Now, Mr. Brown, I'm on a budget. I can't afford to throw out good bread. The rest of the bread is just fine if you cut off the mold."

Mr. Brown, not to appear rude, which is NOT his nature to begin with, took a very slight bight then looked up questionably. "It doesn't have any flavor. You're cooking is either that bad, or that cheap whiskey you fed me has destroyed my taste buds!"

"Could be a combination of both."

There was a knock on Mr. Brown's front door. A knock that sent the teetering pains of Mr. Brown's hangover into a swoon.

"Dad?"

"My son!" Shouted Mr. Brown. "What on earth is that bugger doing here! I have to cover this hole! Dear God, he'll think I'm cured if he sees this hole! Or worse! He'll think I've finally lost it and put me in a medical home!"

"Why, what difference does it make?"

"If he sees this hole he'll be upset! He'll call the landlord! He'll have it patched up! Jesus, I just want them all to just leave me be!"

The Madam smiled. He didn't want to leave her. He didn't want the wall between them restored to its natural state of barrier. He wanted the freedom that came with its opening, maybe not with the rest of the world, but the freedom he had with the Madam.

"That bureau will fit over it!"

"Woman do you think this old body has the strength of Hercules? What kind of fantasies are you having about me????"

"MR. BROWN!"

The knock again with the distant voice asking, "Dad? Dad are you ok?"

Mr. Brown, in a fit, threw the plate of fried fat and such through the hole at the Madam and went for a picture frame on the wall opposite him, fitting it perfectly over the hole.

The Madam leaned in close, her voyeuristic nature taking prominence as she heard the son being let in.

There seemed to be a ritual Mr. Brown had for allowing his son to enter. She could hear the dead bolt on his front door being unlatched, then Mr. Brown screaming, "Not yet!" The Madam then heard Mr. Brown scurry in the distance, then bellow, "Now! You can come in now!"

The door opened then latched again.

"I'm in, Dad."

"Is the door locked behind you?"

"Yes. Is everything ok?"

"Fine, why?"

"You didn't answer when I knocked."

"I didn't answer when you screamed as a baby, but that

didn't seem to mean much either. Why are you here, what do you want?"

"I didn't want to bother you. I just wanted to see if you were ok."

"Why wouldn't I be? I have everything I need."

"I just wanted to be sure. So, how was you're first night or two here?"

"Fine. It was fine. They've been fine."

And for a moment there was silence.

"Is there anything you need while I'm here?"

"Yes. I do need something."

"Oh, sure. Anything. What is it?"

"I need you to leave."

"I could hang this picture for you."

"NO!"

"Dad, I doubt you can hang it yourself."

"Leave it be."

"I respect your need to take care of yourself, but the truth is, you just can't anymore."

"I'M QUITE CAPABLE OF DOING ANYTHING I DAMNED WELL PLEASE! I'm sick and tired of being treated as though I were incapable. You people rarely seemed to understand that the more I'm left alone the more CAPABLE I get! You're all just fucking impediments! Now put that picture down NOW!"

185

"Dad!" The son apparently had moved the painting slightly away from the hole, not seeing the Madam, nor the gaping space in the wall, but still enough to send Mr. Brown reeling with anger.

"Stop it! We had an agreement! You come here at a certain day at a certain time and for the rest of my pleasant days and nights you leave me the alone. NOW GET OUT! You're in my space! You're violating my space! You're ruining my design, my schedule! You're fucking with my habits, do you understand??? It's all tainted now, you hear????"

More moments of silence. The Madam sat on her side of the wall petrified and quiet. She held her hand over her mouth, lest the sound of her heavy breathing should be heard by the son who finally said with bombastic authority, "You either hate me that much you'd yell at me....or you're getting worse like the doctor said you would."

The Madam heard the cold tone of Mr. Brown. "I think its a little bit of both."

She heard only footsteps and the closing of a door.

"Mr. Brown?"

No answer.

"Mr. Brown? are you alright?"

Mr. Brown placed the painting flush against the wall completely sealing it off and said, "I'd like some moments to myself if I may."

She lowered her head, feeling sadness for Mr. Brown,

wishing there was something she could do.

"I understand Mr. Brown. Come fetch me when you feel you're ready. Take all the time you need."

After five weeks, the Madam still had not heard from him....

*   *   *

God knows throughout that time the Madam did her best to spy on him, as was her nature, but the painting pushed up against the wall blocked her entire view. She would often place her ear up against the wall, but what's to hear from a man who sits solitary on a couch for hours on end? Once she thought she heard him cough and that gave her encouragement. "At least he's alive...." Regardless of action or inaction on the other side, she knew he was there and spent her evenings by the hole in the wall just in case he needed her, just in case he decided to pull the painting aside and say a simple, "Hi."

Nightly she slept on that floor, pulling up close to the hole, so close her back brushed aside it, her legs cramping under her from the nightly devotional need to be near him, should he require her. She had thought of moving a deplorably old Queen Anne chair up to the hole to relieve her back of that bad squatting. Alas, the chair, despite it's torn cushions and wrecked back frame was too heavy for her to move. So, the old woman's croaking moans went on as she squdged against the wall.

Weeks of such diligence did take their toll on the Madam. Getting up from the floor had become increasingly difficult. She no longer walked upright on her move to the kitchen or the restroom; the crinkle and cramp on her back having made her hunched and barely able to lift her head past her bosom. Her trips to the market had grown from daily excursions to weekly demands. She carried only what was necessary, often dragging the day old food that was sold to her cheaply in a large canvas bag so she wouldn't have to lift it. At the end of the fifth week the Madam had become practically immobile, unable to move from the floor, unable to even squat anymore, but prone before the hole, her body crying for her to tend to herself, her heart ignoring all warnings, keeping her steadfast, keeping her close to the thought of Mr. Brown's own welfare.

By Saturday of that fifth week she discovered that her whole body had wrenched into one solid painful cramp and still she wouldn't disturb Mr. Brown. Oh, she needed assistance badly, surely. But, whose to say that he would even help her anyway? Their first meeting proved his total inability to leave the confines of his tiny apartment and the Madam was nearly certain that nothing short of a fire would pull him out of there...In some manner she relied on Mr. Brown, for it was generally concluded that he was her only friend. Then again, what friend dismisses you with five weeks of solitude? Some need their space, thought the Madam, and she wouldn't dare curse him for that, nor would she disturb him. She would simply have to wait for him, hope he pulls the painting aside soon to find her totally incapable and.....and what? Who would he call? Surely he wouldn't come in to rescue, so who would he call? The thought of the whole matter depressed her and she went to sleep on the floor again, but this time hungry, for she had been unable to move at all.

By Sunday morning fear had done the old woman no good. She did her best to scrape herself along the floor, but to no avail. Her own weight held her aptly to that spot. She winced against the morning sun and bit her bottom lip for as long as she could delay the issue, but within a matter of time the natural occurrences of the body proved too demanding and the Madam urinated on the floor.

"Oh, GOD!" And slammed went her hand against the floor. "No! NO!" She began to sob, not simply at the embarrassing moment, but at the all around culmination of a tortured, lonely old life.

Then came the voice from the other side of the wall. "Madam?"

"What?" Startled she begged to ask, "Mr. Brown is that you?"

"Don't be silly, of course its me. Who else would it be?"

"Mr. Brown! Oh, thank God, Mr. Brown! It's so good to hear from you!"

Though her back was to the wall, she could hear the painting being pushed aside and the sound of Mr. Brown's voice coming through cleaner.

"Rubbish."

"No! I don't mean to be vain, but I need you desperately!"

"And I, you, Madam."

"What on earth do you need from me?"

"Your whiskey."

"Oh, bother! I'd love to get it for you, but I can't get up, Mr. Brown! I simply can't! I'm an invalid! Look at me!"

She was curled into a position that screamed of pain, her face buried into the wood floor, the urine she was unable to hold for any length freshly soiling her clothes, the warm stink seeping into every crack and crevice of the wood floor that it ran.

"Dear God, woman! What happened?"

"I've not been able to get up for two days."

"Is something wrong?"

"It's my back, I've been sleeping on this floor for over a month!"

"WHAT ON EARTH FOR?"

"In case you needed me."

"But, you're the one who need's assistance, you batty woman!"

"I didn't want to disturb your isolation."

Mr. Brown's heart went shoveling sympathy in heavy

degrees at his feet and he said nothing until she provoked him.

"Mr. Brown, I hate to be a burden....but, I need you desperately."

"For what?"

"For what??? Mr. Brown! I'm trapped on the floor! You must help me up, I beg of you."

"Is there someone I can call for you?" His voice was monotonous and if it did hold any emotion it bordered on the slight shiver of fear. Had she been able to turn her head to him she would have seen a blank eyed stare that revealed the madness that had kept him bound by self imposed isolation for so long.

"Oh, not that again! I knew it!" The Madam was tempestuous, angered. But, by her own desire to comply with Mr. Brown's mental affliction she resisted the need to scream at him and simply sighed. "If I could remind you, Mr. Brown, there is no one....I have *no one*."

Simple phrases have ways of pushing their meaning onto people. To say "I have no one" was not only a declaration of truth, it was also a declaration of disappointment. She may have thought throughout these weeks without hearing from Mr. Brown that he was in fact her only friend, the only single soul that had any importance in her life. Acquaintances at the market never beheld friendships. No one wanted to be her friend, no one wanted to hear how her day was, nor how her health, nor well-being was. She had remained certain Mr. Brown was here for her, would be (or at least COULD be) with a little coaxing.

"You're sure there is no one I could get for you?"

"I told you....I have *no one.*" And she said these words, "*no one*" with such a dramatic sense of brooding that one could feel their total power. She was confessing, reminding, suggesting that she was utterly and shamefully alone. Mr. Brown saw her rest her forehead on the floor and begin to sob ever so quietly.

"Mr. Brown, I like to think myself a lady."

"That's a matter of opinion."

"This is no time for your flirtatious insults. As a lady I find it difficult to tell you...I'm about to soil myself, Mr. Brown."

There was a dreadful silence, the sort that allows everyone the common influence of truth. Mr. Brown considered to himself the human consequences of his actions as he desperately tried to think of the Madam and not himself. He kept staring through that large gaping hole that whiskey had made for them, that a new and quickly honest friendship had made for them, and saw the Madam helpless on the floor, could hear her breathing as she winced trying to hold back the body's need to expel. Mr. Brown remained bound to his own mental inability to move.

"Mr. Brown, please. Hurry."

He moved his mouth as if he were trying to say something, anything. To no avail, that blank-eyed stare kept him tied to a view

192

that was no longer on her, but on a simple step beyond his quiet uninfluenced domain, on the outside world, the criminally influenced, aggressive, angry world. One step through that hole, even if it be to help the one person he felt understood him, was a step outside of the confines of the unyielding, unchanging, deathless world of paranoia he had built for himself.

Even though she had remained in pain by his side should he need her.

"Mr. Brown! PLEASE!"

The outside world was filled with madness, of horrors, of people desperately trying to kill you, poison you, rob you, beat you for your possessions. The outside world was filled with demonic hatred, violence, bitter tongues ready to expose their displeasure with you, incurable diseases that strike at will and with no pattern. The world outside this quiet brown shell was filled with babies that starve, wars with no purpose, beheadings of the innocent to satisfy the hunger of the wicked, disrespect for life, the total governmental and social embrace of murder and.....and the elderly forced to suffer alone in their incontinence and sickness until death comes to take them off the hands of the state.

"Oh, dear God...." Said the madam beginning to sob louder. Mr. Brown could smell what she meant. "This is my life? This is how it ends?" She was crying badly, and often times what she said was unintelligible, but Mr. Brown could hear things like, "to die shitting myself on the floor? Starving to death. No one to help me. I have *no one*."

"Why would you die?" Asked Mr. Brown.

"I've been on this floor for two days...I haven't been able to eat! I've grown content with pissing on the floor, but shitting myself was intolerable! It's embarrassing."

"Starving ought to be better than eating your food. Its a much more humane way to die, don't you think?"

"HOW DARE YOU! I'VE HAD ENOUGH ALREADY! I WON'T TOLERATE THIS ANYMORE!"......was what she *thought*, was what she *wanted* to scream, and indeed the need to do so was so great it nearly gave her the strength to rise to her feet and rush through that hole and beat the old Mr. Brown to a bloody stump. But, she resisted....she still contented to comply with his illness...despite what may happen to her. And why? This is the mystery of human connection. We fight often our own needs in order to satisfy those we see as the surplus of our deficit. Instead of screaming she whispered, "You're a thorn in my side, you old bastard. Its a damned good thing you've decided to shut yourself up so the rest of us could be left alone. That breath of yours is enough to make me want to call the landlord AND REPAIR THAT HOLE IN THE WALL!"

"Ha! Fat chance! You can't get him to come and fix the toilet! But, you don't need one of those though, do you?"

Stung, it did. Stung enough to cause her to let a few tears go, let them shrink down the cheek without him neither seeing nor hearing her do so. It was cruel to say such a thing, but she was willing to play this game if it meant helping not herself, but him.

"As soon as I'm up off this floor you're likely to get a good striking from me."

"I probably deserve it. As far as I'm concerned if someone hate's me, I've given them good reason."

Now, here, be sure to say how much you hate him, how much you were so hoping he'd help you, because you've been so devoted to him....

"I don't hate you, Mr. Brown."

"You should."

"I understand you too well to hate you."

"You don't understand me, don't try and say that you do."

"Oh, I do. I may not understand what you're going through or what causes you to disappear into a room for good....but, I do understand that's who you are and there is no changing that. And why would I want to change it? You're like a goldfish for a voyeur like me. You swim around in your little apartment doing nothing extraordinary, but the simple fact that you're there is enough to give me pleasure. Why would I want that to end? Why would I want that to ever be different? Why would I want you to be any different."

He was afraid now to speak.

195

Neither of them said another word to each other for the rest of the day. However, they both stayed exactly where they were. Even Mr. Brown, still physically functioning, could not bring himself to move. He couldn't remove his eyes from the dreadful sight of the Madam, pained, moaning on occasion, lying in her own filth. His mind had gone numb to thought, relevant thought, that is. His mind still harking the coming warning of an attempt to help her, for if he did, he would step into that world he hated so....*But she was there for you, throughout these many weeks in case you needed her.* And he would have remained in that catatonic daze had she not spoke.

"Sunset is coming and I'm afraid....I'm afraid I'll have to ask you to call the landlord to come help me off my feet....or an ambulance. And if either of them come, they'll see the hole in the wall, think we're dangerous and violent people and kick one of us out. Probably me. I'm accustomed to causing the state money."

"Or?"

"Or I die here starving to death on the floor."

"Where will you go? If I call the landlord or an ambulance....where will you go?"

....in case you need her.

"You think old women pushing carts on the street do it cause they WANT to????"

Mr. Brown now took to crouching, so that the war that split

196

his emotions inside him could fight it out with either a leap through the hole, or a hesitant rest and denial.

"I'm going to sleep now, Mr. Brown."

The sun had passed its last rays through the nicotine stained window panes that bordered her front room. The squares they painted on the floor moved close to the Madam's hard and worn body in shades that waned from brilliant orange to sullen gray. But, hush....said the world, and neither Mr. Brown nor the Madam said a thing.

He didn't move, he rested crouched as mentioned, deeper and deeper in thought. The air grew darker around the two of them. Night claimed its prominence and darkness pushed itself into every corner. The Madam barely breathed, and when she did, he could hear it. A hoarse breath that labored its way in and out. On occasion she coughed, but winced at the pain the pressure caused on her back, then rushed back swiftly into slumber.

The outside world, Mr. Brown, is filled with rotten people and moments. The outside world is deceitful and untrusting.

She's in this position because of you....She's been sitting there on the floor waiting for you *in case you need her*....Whatever happens to her, be it death or homelessness, shall be due to your inaction, Mr. Brown. And you didn't even need to be in the outside world for that to happen, you simply *are*, you *exist*, and therefore, you're life, no matter how shut up, has consequences, has

197

connections to life. Life is never completely without connection. Destiny will make sure of that. Besides, Mr. Brown....don't you care? Don't you care what may happen to her? You have your isolation...and at the same time, someone inclined to accept you *as is*. Such a rarity....And you're inaction will take that away. If you call an ambulance she'll be done for....and if you leave her there, she'll be done for....But, you could rescue her, for all you have do is finally connect with her....again, you can be the surplus of her deficit....as she has been yours. Because, despite your need to be free of the smoking groan of a dying, helpless, pitiful world, *you need her*.

He put his hand on the broken edge of the hole in the wall and leaned his head forward, then quickly retracted with fear. And as if she could have possibly heard his thoughts the Madam said through a whisper, "I'm only a step away, Mr. Brown. Just start by reaching out your hand."

"How did you know I was still here?"

"I'm a voyeur. I can hear that you've never left....and that you're holding the wall."

"I'm trying, Madam. I'm trying."

"I know you are. Take you're time...."

"I don't want to leave this place."

"I don't want to either. I like it here....now that you're here."

"Everyone thinks I'm crazy."

"But, you are, Mr. Brown. You're psychotic and mad...and I love you for it.....You can come in quickly, help me to my feet so I may get to the chair, then I can recover and hopefully make my way to the kitchen. But, if you can just get me to my feet you can rush back through the hole and I'll be fine."

"Are you sure?"

"I'm sure. Five minutes tops."

With the precision and mannered detailed afforded those who are obsessive compulsive, Mr. Brown dashed through the window with an agility and speed that defied his elder years. His breath was manic, his sweat quickly spilling down his shirt, the fine gray hairs on the back of his neck prickly, as if they were reaching back to the solace of his little apartment. Mr. Brown slowly raised the Madam from her upper torso into his arms in a fashion similar to that of a hug as she utilized the movement to thank him, grabbing a tight hold around his back. "Thank you, Mr. Brown! Well done! God bless you! God bless you! I owe you all my whiskey!" She giggled through joyful tears. But, Mr. Brown would show no sentiment. At least not yet.

"Up on your feet old woman! Up I say!"

"Just to the chair, then I'll be fine."

"I don't want to be blamed for having you sit in your own shit! Up, I said! Off your feet! I'm taking you to the bath."

She looked at him with that demure demeanor the rescued are

inclined to give their heroes.

His strength was unusual for an idle man who sat so often, who did nothing for physical exercise, for he swept the lofty Madam boldly up off her feet with an ease that seemed ridiculous to him and rushed her to the bathtub. Softly he set her inside the slightly mildewed tub as she said, "I'm overwhelmed, Mr. Brown. I don't know how to thank you."

"You can agree never to feed me your horrible cooking again."

She laughed and said, "Anything you desire, Mr. Brown."

"Speaking of your food....Do you have soup?"

"I haven't had a chance to get the market. There's nothing in the pantry."

"Oh that market! You shouldn't shop there!"

"Its what I can afford."

"Can you get yourself undressed? I don't think I have the stomach to see you naked just now."

"Oh, well thank you!" she said sarcastically, then smiled. "I can undress myself fine."

"Take a bath, then. I'll be back shortly."

Mr. Brown went back through the hole into his own apartment and went to his kitchen, well stocked with well made food and not the sort the Madam was forced to consume on a budget of food vouchers handed reluctantly to her by the state. He pulled out some beef, some carrots, some potatoes and commenced to make a quick hearty stew and while it brewed he went to his telephone.

Resilience in life can push a man to do what survival deems natural. "Son?"

"I'm surprised to hear you."

"I don't like interrogation so just listen to me carefully."

"Ok."

"I apologize. I don't think I need to say anything else. I've said it, its done."

Mr. Brown could hear his son on the other side say, "For?"

"Oh, don't be ninny, boy! For whatever it applies to! Just take it, run with it, do what you want with it!"

"Accepted."

"Now, do me something, boy. Something very important."

"What?"

"The groceries you send by once a month."

"Yes."

"Double the order on everything."

"Why?"

"Again with the questions. I don't like to explain myself, you know. I feel like eating more! Perhaps my condition has worsened into schizophrenia and now I'm eating for two! Don't make me pull out my other personality. He's more an ass than I am!"

"Very well."

"It is my money and I can spend it like I wish. Hell, why bother with you, I can call the grocer myself and have him deliver it to me without you, anyway."

"Then why don't you?"

"Don't make me get sappy, you shit.....It's the only chance I get to see you."

"I could always come by more-"

"Nope. I like it once a month just fine. Just once a month is all I need."

"I'll double the order."

"I have to go. My stew is about to burn."

"I was wanting to talk to you about-"

"I have to go, son. No time for emotional chit chat. Tell you're wife I think she's fat."

"DAD!"

Mr. Brown hung up the phone.

The stew would have been better slowly drawn over the course of a few hours, naturally, but he didn't have that much time. So he allowed it to simmer while he went back through the hole into the Madam's apartment.

At the bathroom door he knocked. "Have you drowned, yet?"

"The hot water is good for my back and feels wonderful.

Should I drowned, it would be a marvelous way to go. I feel fantastic."

He only smiled then moved into her bedroom.

The room was cluttered with trash, but not the sort you and I find worthy of tossing. It was a bit of this and a bit of that which could one day or another find itself useful to someone with no money and no resources. A scarp of yarn, a few tattered blank envelopes, scores of jars, some empty, some holding discarded buttons. Mr. Brown was investigating the bed. As he suspected, it was a cheaply worn thing. A mattress, sunk in the middle, but sitting on a simple detachable metal frame.

As he disassembled the mattress from the frame he could smell the stew. The potatoes were nearly soft enough, the meat just about tender.

Down the scrawny hall, with just a scratch or two being summoned on the wall, (to which he nearly winced, until he remembered the hollow they had bludgeoned in the wall) the entire bed was moved and placed flush aside the hole in the wall.

"Mr. Brown???? What on earth is that racket???"

"I despise your apartment, Madam. Its dreadful."

"I beg your pardon?"

"Do you need help getting out of the tub?"

"I think I do. If you could find my bathrobe in my bedroom and toss it in, I'd be most grateful."

Mr. Brown found the tattered thing, splotchy from years of age, holes beginning to form around the bottom. With a slight crack in the door Mr. Brown tossed the robe into the bathroom, it landing easily on the floor where the Madam could reach it.

The Madam, having cleansed herself, drained the water from the tub, dried herself while still in the confines of the porcelain, then redressed herself with the robe with only some slight discomfort.

"Mr. Brown? I'm ready now."

The old woman was helped from the tub and down the slight hall to the living room. "Ought I go to my bed?" She asked Mr. Brown as he honestly replied, "You are going to your bed and for God's sakes stay in it until you recover."

Upon seeing the bed aligned against the hole in the wall tears began to swell in her eyes. She cupped her hand over her mouth to hide the dreadful twist a cry can cause a smile. "Oh, Mr. Brown...."

"I'll put you here for a while....In case you need me."

The Madam was laid in bed carefully, as Mr. Brown wormed his way around her and crawled through his hole in the wall. The bed was just at the bottom edge of the hole, leaving more than enough room for them to enjoy each other's company.

Mr. Brown pulled cushions from his couch and placed them through the hole so the Madam could sit nearly upright. He then handed her a bowl of his stew saying, "If you haven't eaten in two days, stew is best for you. The liquid nutrients will get into your blood faster, help you get your strength back." And all this time the Madam could say nothing, lest it be stuttered with joyful sobbing.

"What are you waiting for? Eat up! I'll be back in a moment."

The stew was wonderfully rich and flavorful, filled with the aromatic blessing of sage and fresh vegetables, a beef that seemed seasoned with cracked pepper and cabernet and heated to just the perfect degree. The Madam closed her eyes after the first bight to savor its homey, hearty comfort.

Now, Mr. Brown was not done with his surprises, heavens no. His bed, not unlike the simple metal frame of the Madam's, but with a much sturdier mattress, was dismantled and replaced against the hole on his side of the wall.

"I would have given you my mattress, Madam," said he comfortably arranging himself into bed, "but I don't think it would fit through this hole!"

*You could have taken it out the front door and into my....*But, she stopped that thought immediately. "I'm so proud of you, Mr. Brown. So very proud. The soup is delicious, by the way!"

"I do fancy myself a very good cook."

"I'll say!"

Then she thought to herself, do you dare ask him why he cringed away for so long? For five weeks? Aren't you desperate to know? Alas, the compassionate tolerance that is so uniquely the

Madam's and not the common man's did not yield itself to interrogate. She allowed him the mystery of being who he is distinctly, without being combative, obtrusive, nor provoking. Besides, the romantic notion of his rescue and now his help with her recovery was the issue here. It was splendid and complete with smiles and joy.

She said, "I do believe I'll no longer cook for you, Mr. Brown."

"Thank, God. One more dish off your menu and I'll be obliged to call an ambulance!"

"But, I do want to thank you, Mr. Brown, for your kindness, for your help."

"You have, Madam."

She need not ask why. Her deplorable sleeping on the floor aside the hole these many weeks was the thankful gesture he referred to.

"Now, I'll be cooking for you, Madam."

"Oh, do say! Why, that's most kind."

"And you can supply the whiskey."

"Seems like a very fair trade!"

"You'll get the good stuff. There's a respectable Irish whiskey. Jameson's. You'll be getting that from now on."

"Awfully expensive, isn't it?"

"If you're not paying for food, then you can afford the

whiskey."

She smiled and said, "It's a deal."

"And what ever is left over at the end of the month, you put away in a drawer and save it. Well, all this rushing about and rearranging furniture has made me tired."

"It is late."

"Shall I take your bowl for you?"

"Yes, please."

The bowl was passed through the hole into Mr. Brown's hands and returned to the kitchen as the Madam positioned herself comfortably in bed. Lights on Mr. Brown's side were turned off and he, too, scurried under his covers. How remarkable it was, the heads of both beds were identically aside one another on either side of the hole. Had there not been a wall there, they may very well have been in the same bed.

They both sighed as they comforted themselves into rest, and tenderly Mr. Brown reached through the hole and placed his hand upon the Madam's shoulder.

"Good night, Madam."

"Good night, Mr. Brown."

And she smiled to herself, reached over and placed her hand on his and told herself with the confidence of a very wealthy woman,

I have someone....

www.ingramcontent.com/pod-product-compliance
Lightning Source LLC
Chambersburg PA
CBHW030324020726
47493CB00004B/1158